FORDS AND FLYING MACHINES

MY STORY series

In chronological order:

ON BOARD THE BOUSSOLE,
the Diary of Julienne Fulbert,
Lapérouse's Voyage of Discovery,
1785-1788
by Christine Edwards

SURVIVING SYDNEY COVE,
the Diary of Elizabeth Harvey,
Sydney, 1790
by Goldie Alexander

THE RUM REBELLION,
the Diary of David Bellamy,
Sydney Town, 1807–1808
by Libby Gleeson

A BANNER BOLD,
the Diary of Rosa Aarons,
Ballarat Goldfield, 1854
by Nadia Wheatley

THE YANKEE WHALER,
the Diary of Thomas Morris,
Bunbury WA, 1876
by Deborah Lisson

PLAGUES AND FEDERATION,
the Diary of Kitty Barnes,
The Rocks, Sydney, 1900
by Vashti Farrer

A DIFFERENT SORT OF REAL,
the Diary of Charlotte McKenzie,
Melbourne, 1918-1919
by Kerry Greenwood

WHO AM I?
the Diary of Mary Talence,
Sydney, 1937
by Anita Heiss

THE BOMBING OF DARWIN,
the Diary of Tom Taylor,
1942
by Alan Tucker

A TALE OF TWO FAMILIES,
the Diary of Jan Packard,
Melbourne, 1974
by Jenny Pausacker

MY STORY

FORDS AND FLYING MACHINES

THE DIARY OF JACK McLAREN

LONGREACH, 1919–1921

by Patricia Bernard

A Scholastic Press book from Scholastic Australia

My 'every lasting' thanks to Mr Gary Deakin, curator of the Powerhouse Museum, Longreach; George Roberts, curator of Qantas Historical Museum, Mascot; Bob Alford, Darwin Heritage Consultant; Colin Julin; and to my patient editor, Katinka Proudfoot.
Thank you friends.

LEXILE™ 1060

Scholastic Press
345 Pacific Highway
Lindfield NSW 2070
an imprint of Scholastic Australia Pty Limited (ABN 11 000 614 577)
PO Box 579, Gosford NSW 2250.
www.scholastic.com.au

Part of the Scholastic Group
Sydney ● Auckland ● New York ● Toronto ● London ● Mexico City
● New Delhi ● Hong Kong ● Puerto Rico ● Buenos Aires

First published by Scholastic Press in 2003.

Cover design by Antart, Sydney.

Reprinted in 2004.

National Library of Australia Cataloguing-in-Publication entry
Bernard, Patricia.
Fords and flying machines: the diary of Jack McLaren, Longreach. 1919-1921.
For 8-12 year old children.
ISBN 1 86504 562 4.
1. Qantas Airways – Juvenile fiction. 2.Airlines – Queensland – History.
3. Airlines – Northern Territory – History. I. Title. (Series: My Story)
A823.3

Typeset in Usherwood and Frizz Quadrata.

Printed by McPherson's Printing Group, Victoria.

10 9 8 7 6 5 4 3 2 4 5 6 / 0

In the early twentieth century, people used certain words and expressions that are no longer considered appropriate. For instance, Jack uses *blackfella* and *blacks* to describe Indigenous Australians and *Chinaman* or *Oriental* to talk about Chinese Australians. Some people might find these words derogatory or offensive, but they are not meant to be so.

Some of the placenames in the diary have now changed: Burma is now called Myanmar; the Dutch East Indies is now Indonesia; Batavia is modern-day Jakarta; Constantinople is now called Istanbul; and Persia is now known as Iran.

The Diary of Jack McLaren

1919–1921

And he sees the vision splendid
of the sunlit plains extended,
And at night the wondrous glory
of the everlasting stars.

Banjo Patterson

5 August 1919—Central Station, Sydney

Dear Matt, or Miss Matilda McLaren, as Mama says I must call you now you have turned fourteen.

As promised I have started my diary-letter to you immediately. Please save all the pages.

I miss you already. It was so sad seeing Mama and Pa disappearing in a cloud of steam at Central Station and sad that you weren't there to wave me off.

Mama said that Mrs Wentworth couldn't spare you as she was having guests. That started Pa rocking back and forth on his crutches and fuming into his beard about how he hadn't braved the four oceans and crossed the wide world, from freezing Scotland to boiling Australia, to have some hoity-toity madam tell his daughter what to do; when the same hoity-toity madam wasn't good enough to lick his daughter's bootstraps.

Mama hushed him but I laughed. It was good to see him with his dander up and not feeling downhearted as he has been since his accident.

So dear twin, we shall have to make do with our last goodbye. Wasn't it fun at the tram yards? Who would have thought that a cable tram's engine and brake system worked that way? Trust you to figure it out. The tram mechanic's face was a picture when you told him. And how more surprised he was when I explained that you only knew about machines because you were born first, and had I been the firstborn, I would have been the one to answer all his questions. Thank you for the elbow in the ribs. They still hurt.

Pa was extraordinarily proud of you when I told him how impressed the mechanic was. I heard him telling Mama that you could have been an engineer if we lived in Europe, because there are women engineers there.

Of course she answered with, 'But can she use a Singer sewing machine to make a fine seam?'

I said you could if you didn't hate sewing so much.

Which brings me to how sorry I am that you are not coming with me to become an apprentice in Cousin George's garage. It isn't fair that you have to be a housemaid while I get to fiddle with machines as much as I like.

So I have made a vow. When I'm finished my apprenticeship, and have saved enough, I will buy a garage and you will be my partner. Then you can fiddle with machines until you are up to your wrists in oil and have it dripping off your nose, if you like.

Mind, Mama may be correct in saying that no decent young man is going to settle for a young lady with fingernails full of grease. But then, if a decent young lady can settle for my fingernails, I don't see why an 'enlightened man' (to quote Pa) can't settle for yours.

Which brings me to my second vow. I shall tell you everything I learn about machines. That way you won't feel so bad about having to wash mountains of dishes or polish thousands of stairs every week.

I shall begin with the Brisbane Express. It is a splendid train with a magnificent steam locomotive, six first- and second-class carriages and a guard's van. The first-class sleepers have maroon velvet plush seats, tons of shiny brass (imagine polishing that every week?) and beautifully etched glass doors. I saw them when we stopped for four minutes at a country station called Broadmeadows.

What a mad rush that was. Everyone was out in the corridor and onto the platform in a flash, all pushing and hurrying to buy meat pies and cups of tea. The queue was so long that some people had not been served when the guard's bell rang, causing a second scramble to board before he waved his green flag, and the train pulled out.

Second class (where I am seated, and sorry if my writing is bad but the train is rocking) is very comfortable with horsehair-stuffed leather seats and a plain glass sliding door. I share this compartment with two cattle agents, both wearing tweed suits and waistcoats looped with gold Albert watch chains and fobs.

One told me that we will reach Wallangarra, which is on the Queensland border, at 7.45 tomorrow morning, when we will change trains. This is because New South Wales's rail gauge is 1 foot 2½ inches wider than Queensland's. He thinks it's stupid to have two different-sized train lines. I think so too. Imagine catching the tram from Sydney Central Station to Leichhardt and having to change trams at each suburb's border. We would never reach home.

The first man blamed the Queensland Government. The second, who is a Queenslander, became red in the face and blamed the New South Wales Government. With each of them waving their cigars around and puffing angrily, our compartment was soon so full of smoke, I could hardly breathe.

After Newcastle, the men began arguing about who was to blame for the influenza epidemic that has killed over ten thousand Australians.

The Queenslander said the germs were brought back by the soldiers returning from the Great War. The New South Wales man said they came from the foreign ships in the docks. He also said that over thirty thousand people had been inoculated, himself included.

We know about that, don't we Matt? I shall remember the smell of the iodine and the pain of the hypodermic syringe forever, and I am still wearing the bag of camphor Mama made for me around my neck. Not to mention her prayers. It would be a very strong influenza germ that managed to get past those.

After we left Tamworth, the New South Wales man began describing a film he'd seen at a Sydney theatre called *The Sentimental Bloke.* Next minute he was reciting to me the poetry that the film was based on. I didn't want to be rude and say that I knew the poem because my father read CJ Dennis's poems to us.

Do you remember when we performed the Romeo, Juliet, Ginger Mick and Doreen scene, sitting on the top of our tin roof in our bathing costumes, yelling as loud as we could? Mrs Doreen Lack was threatening to throw buckets of water over us if we didn't stop shouting her name to the world. Luckily she couldn't reach us, but I remember the whack I got from Pa's shaving strop when we came down.

Now the men are talking about their job, which is to buy up the mobs of cattle and sheep that the drovers bring to the railheads, ship them to Sydney and Melbourne, and sell them for a great profit.

The New South Wales man said there were seventeen million sheep in Queensland and he intends buying all of them, eventually.

The Queensland man said he already had a contract for a herd of ten thousand head of cattle, all from a station called Tinnenburra. He is boasting that in Sydney the cattle will be worth 15 pounds a head and that his commission will be 'very nice, thank you'. It's hard to believe that one man can own ten thousand cattle, and that a cow is worth as much as Pa once earned a month.

My hand is tiring, so I will tell you a secret. The night before I left Sydney, I crept into Mrs Wentworth's garden to say goodbye. I planned to tap on your window, but I couldn't find the servants' quarters, so I left you two presents. For the first one, you must dig under the third rosebush from the gate. Hope you like it.

Try to visit Mama and Pa as often as Mrs Wentworth will allow. With us both gone and Pa a cripple, it is going to be hard for them. Mama says they have saved enough. But I don't see how.

6 August 1919—Queensland border

What a journey! What a night! I thought it would never end. Although, it was interesting travelling through the high country around Armidale, and seeing the immense forests and rolling green hills, dotted with dairy and beef-cattle farms. But it was too cold to sleep, and my thin jacket didn't help.

The Queenslander boasted that it would be hotter than hell in Longreach, which, he said, was beyond the black stump and a godforsaken hole to boot. He wanted to know why a city lad like myself was going there.

I explained that my mother's cousin, a Mr George Gorham, worked as a mechanic for the Longreach Motor Company, and that he had acquired a mechanic's apprenticeship for me there; and that Pa thought it a great chance for me.

'Oh aye,' he agreed, puffing away at a huge cigar. 'A mechanical apprenticeship is the way to go. Machines are taking over the world. Look at them flying machines they had in the Great War. Fancy being shot at by one of those.'

I told him I thought most flying machines shot at other flying machines. But he said he'd heard that in Palestine, flying machines followed roads and shot up people. It gave him nightmares thinking about it. He would never trust a flying machine; they would never take the place of coaches, trains and boats; and if God had meant us to fly he'd have given us wings.

I was tempted to add that if God had wanted

man to smoke he'd have given him a chimney and not a nose, but I didn't. However I have decided never to smoke cigarettes, cigars or a pipe, even if it is manly.

Later—Roma Street Station, Brisbane

When the Wallangarra train arrived at Brisbane, everything became chaotic, with shouting porters carrying cases, people greeting people, people losing people, people rushing back and forth looking for people; while beyond the platform lights, everything was pitch black, even though it was only 9 pm.

I felt lost for a bit, then I showed a ticket guard the label Mama had hung around my neck (I had taken it off, as I felt like a parcel). He directed me to the Rockhampton Mail 21A which is due to leave in an hour, and so I am writing to you while I wait.

The train from Wallangarra to Brisbane is one of Queensland's most prestigious trains, even though it rocked more than the train from Sydney due to its tracks being of a narrower gauge. During this stretch, I was in a compartment with an elderly lady who shared her breakfast sandwiches with me, as I had eaten everything Mama packed.

What strange sandwiches, Matt! They were made of pickled kangaroo tail. The old lady said she pickled it herself, and that she preferred it to pickled possum which, she said, tasted like cat, didn't I agree?

I replied that I had never tasted pickled cat, possum or kangaroo tail.

'Then eat up,' she ordered.

So I did. Kangaroo tail tastes salty.

I hope Mrs Wentworth is treating you well. And yes, I am homesick and a bit scared. The money Mama gave me is hidden in my shoe, along with two shilling pieces the cattle agents gave me and sixpence the old lady gave me for being a brave boy.

I am going to post these pages with the tuppenny stamps Pa gave me.

Love, Jack.

7 August 1919—Gateway to the Cattle Country

Dear Matt,

Did you like my secret? The shopkeeper said it was the best brand of screwdriver in the world.

I am tired and dirty. Every time someone opens the window, dust, ash and cinders fly in. Once again I have travelled all night and all day sitting up. I awoke when the Rockhampton Mail stopped at Bundaberg to drop off mail and to allow the passengers to alight for breakfast. I was starving, as I had not eaten since yesterday morning.

The Railway Refreshment Room's tables were set with damask tablecloths, fine china and heavy silver cutlery, but this was for the first-class passengers. We second-classers stood at a linoleum-covered counter to drink our tea out of cups with rims as thick as my thumb. I had a scone and a sausage roll. It did not fill me up.

The man beside me poured his tea into his saucer and blew on it exactly the way Mama says we mustn't. He winked at me, then rubbed my hair. He said he was going to a horse race and he would need a bit of red-hair luck.

When the train stopped for lunch at Gladstone, I didn't go into the Refreshment Room because two sailors on their way to the port of Rockhampton shared their meat pies with me. One brought me a cup of tea. He handed it through the window telling me to 'Guzzle up afore you're spied by the lassie. Seconds are free as long as the first cuppa is paid for.'

People are very kind but they ask a lot of questions, so I have had to explain about Pa's accident at the railway yards, Mama having to stay home and tutor students instead of teaching at school, and you having to become a skivvy. They are most sympathetic.

The sailors are playing poker and drinking rum. They slap the cards down on an upturned suitcase and are making a lot of noise. The guard has been in twice to tell them to be quiet otherwise he will order them off the train, even if it means stopping mid-station. They aren't the slightest bit afraid.

They told me that at Rockhampton they are joining a ship bound for Shanghai, where they will ride around in rickshaws and cross the mighty Yangtze River in four-storied paddle steamers. One day we shall travel the world and ride in a rickshaw, Matt. I promise.

Later—Rockhampton

We arrived at Rockhampton passenger terminal at 4 pm. I was told by a railway worker that he was working on a new rail line that was to continue north to Townsville. This line is to go along Denison Street, a street that goes straight through the middle of the town. Fancy having a train passing by your front door.

With five hours to wait, I left my bag with the stationmaster and went to explore the town and quay. The houses are made of wood and built on stilts to catch the breeze, as it is hot here all year. The port, which is a good half hour's hike, is not a seaport but the Quay Street-Fitzroy River Port. It is full of cargo ships from all over the world, filling up their holds with sugar, bananas and beef.

I was looking at a ship, when two foreign-looking sailors grabbed me under the arms and began hauling me up its gangplank. Fortunately, the stationmaster had warned me about how young lads are often shanghaied and forced to work as cabin boys on foreign ships, so I struggled hard, kicked one in the shins, and yelled so loudly that they dropped me. I scrambled down the gangplank and raced for the safety of the goods and cargo station, minus my new cap. Imagine Matt, I might have been kidnapped and taken to China.

I told the stationmaster and he said it was because of my red hair; sailors believe that a ship will not sink as long as there is a redhead on board. Then he became serious and said, 'Let that be a lesson to you, sonny.'

Now I am sitting on a goods platform, watching ten men load a huge pine-wood crate onto a goods train. A guard said the crate came across the Pacific Ocean from Canada and that there will be a queue of people waiting for it when it is unpacked, as Oregon pine makes beautiful flooring.

He said the crate holds the makings of a Model T Ford—engine, chassis and wheels—and it is going to the Longreach railhead, which is where most of the Model T Fords that arrive in Rockhampton go.

Just being this close to the workingman's motorcar is exciting. I wonder if I will learn mechanics on this one.

8 August 1919—On the way west

I am writing this on the last leg of my journey on a number 344, PB15 class train. When I get off, I don't care if I never see another train again. The seats are hard and the window sash is broken, so the window will not go up, which means more grit, cinders and smoke.

The days up here are much hotter than Sydney but the nights are cold. I have been shivering for hours. When I reach Longreach I shall sleep for a week, unless I am meant to start apprenticing immediately.

My travelling companions this time are two rouseabouts, Bert and Snowy. Bert confessed, rather red-faced, that he had been to Brisbane to get hitched (married), but due to the Queensland Railway rules prohibiting men and women travelling together in the same compartment, his new wife, a city girl who is to become the companion-help to the station-owner's wife, has to travel in the women's carriage.

'She's a timid little thing,' he said, even more red-faced.

'Then she won't last long in the outback,' said the other rouseabout.

The train stopped at Emerald around midnight to take on water and again at Barcaldine at dawn, where I saw camels for the first time.

A dark-skinned man was riding one and leading a pack camel. They trotted up to the train, two dark shadows, with the pink sky behind them. Then, slowly, they plodded past my open window as if looking for someone.

Tom told me the camel rider was an Afghani called Ali Baba and that he was once the local postman for the distant cattle stations. Rumour has it that Ali Baba wrote off to India for a wife who reached Brisbane but never arrived in Barcaldine. Now he comes to meet each train in search of her.

Imagine getting your wife by mail order and your letters by camel. They are such odd creatures, Matt. Quite ugly, with slobbering, hairy lips and a long, purple tongue, and they dribble. I can't believe my favourite war hero, Lawrence of Arabia, rides one.

Bert says that blacks, kangaroos and wallabies won't drink at waterholes that camels frequent.

Cattle don't care for them either and will often stampede if they come too close. He said that there were twelve thousand camels in Australia.

I asked him if he'd heard of Lawrence of Arabia. He raised his eyebrows and answered, 'You mean the bloke who saved Britain's bacon?'

Later, as we were leaving Barcaldine, Bert pointed to a string of ghost gums and told me that it was there, in 1891, that his grandfather had joined the Great Shearers' Strike.

'One thousand shearers downed clippers and refused to shear one more of the state's seventeen million sheep until they got better wages and better conditions from the rich graziers,' he said.

'Did they get better conditions?' I asked.

'Not fast enough,' said Tom, who seemed to know as much about the strike as Bert. 'So some of the shearers burnt down the shearing sheds. The Government declared this treason and threw them in jail. That made the shearers angry, so they formed the Australian Labor Party. Then the graziers, who called the shearers "Communists", formed the United Australia Party, which is now called the Country Party. And that's how Australia got its political parties.'

Bert said that another shearers' strike was looming and that I should keep my eyes peeled. I said I would. Although I am not sure what I am looking for. A lot of angry men waving sheep shearing clippers, I suppose.

Bert and Tom slept with their broadbrimmed hats over their faces, but I couldn't sleep. The train kept stopping all along the 400 mile track. When no-one was at these windswept sidings in the middle of nowhere, the guard left the parcels sitting beside the line with a note attached to them. Imagine doing that in Sydney?

9 August 1919—Longreach

George Gorham was waiting on Longreach Station. I was glad to see him; I was tired of travelling. What surprised me was that he knew Bert and Tom. He said everyone knows everyone up here.

He doesn't look like Mama. He has bushy eyebrows and a stern, sunburnt face, and he wears his hat pulled down so far you can't see his blue eyes. His first words to me were that he had no time for lazy whippersnappers or grubby guttersnipes and that he hoped I wasn't one of them.

I told him that at fourteen, I was neither a whippersnapper nor a guttersnipe; that I had good references and intended making a success of myself; and I was only grubby because I'd been travelling on trains for four days.

He grunted at this. Grunting is Cousin George's way of talking.

As we left the station he rounded on me and told me that we were going on a fool's errand (although I had no idea what fool's errand he was talking about); that a year earlier a group, riding motorcycles with sidecars, led by a bloke called Reginald Lloyd, had set off in search of an air service route across Australia and nothing had come of it; and nothing would come of this tomfoolery.

I wanted to ask, 'What tomfoolery? What air service route?' But he was in a hurry to get me settled, so I figured it would all come out in the wash. Either that or Cousin George wasn't the full quid.

Cousin George, or George, as he says I am to call him, has a motorcycle without a sidecar, so I rode on the pillion seat, hanging onto my bag and him. It was a bumpy ride. Longreach's roads are made of dirt, with big potholes in them. He took me to the Methodist Mission hostel where I am to board with a Mrs Banks, as he boards at the Commercial Hotel.

The Methodist Mission boards a lot of young boys. There is George Avery (called Avery as there are too many Georges in Longreach). He is fourteen and also an apprentice mechanic. Within minutes of my announcing that I was to become an apprentice, he was skiting about how he knew everything there was to know about Model T Fords; that he was saving up to buy one; and that they cost 114 pounds.

I told him I couldn't imagine having that much money or owning my own automobile.

I share Avery's room. It has a mirror over the mantlepiece, an ornate metal ceiling and floral leadlights in the windows. Mrs Banks, who is about as old as Mama, said it was once the dining room of a big house that had belonged to a rich lady who'd left it to the mission in her will.

There are four of us in this room. The other two boys, Greg and Paul Jenkins, are younger. They are from a cattle station way out in the Georgina River country on the Northern Territory border. They board here while they go to school and go home during school holidays. They know everything about horses, fencing, and cattleduffing (that's when another station owner, drover, or thief grabs your unbranded cattle, brands them with his own brand and sells them).

I shall post this tomorrow. Now to tell you where my second goodbye present is buried. Dig on the left side of Mrs Wentworth's wisteria, the deep purple one in the front garden.

Love, Jack.

11 August 1919—Methodist Mission hostel

Dear Matt,

Yesterday I was too busy getting settled and visiting the Longreach Motor Company to write. Did you like your second present? Pa said a good wrench is worth a king's ransom.

Mrs Banks insists all boys wash their own clothes and bathe in cold water six days a week. On Sunday we get a hot bath.

I also have chores. I must bring in the firewood for the stove and fill the woodbox in the scullery for the copper, which is used to boil sheets and towels, and I must carpet-sweep the main room once a week.

Greg's and Paul's job is to be up early to collect a billy of milk from the dairyman, who delivers it to the house in two big aluminium milk cans, carried in a billygoat cart.

Avery's job is to collect the meat from the butcher's cart and to keep Mrs Banks's Kosciusko ice chest full of ice. The ice comes with the butcher in his horsedrawn cart. So three times a week, Avery has to carry the huge sixpenny blocks of ice on his shoulder from the cart to the kitchen without dropping them.

In return, the butcher gives him all the ice chips

he wants. Avery is very popular. There is nothing better than sucking on a chip of ice when it's hot.

12 August 1919—Longreach Motor Company

Now I know what George was talking about, and he is the full quid. We, as he has refused to leave me behind, are to travel from Longreach, Queensland, to Katherine, in the Northern Territory, on a survey job for the Department of Defence.

The survey is to find the best route for an air race being run by the government. When they say 'route' they actually mean where the airstrips will be built for the aircraft to land and refuel. These must be no more than 300 to 350 air miles apart, otherwise the aircraft will run out of fuel and crash. I can hardly believe my luck.

Avery is most put out that he wasn't chosen, as he is the town's oldest apprentice. Because he is so jealous he held me under the water in the bath this evening. I thought I would drown, but Greg, Paul and two other boys jumped on his back and forced him to let me go.

Later on he said he was sorry and that he'd only done it because the men we will be travelling with, Mr McGinness and Mr Fysh, are his heroes.

He knows all about them and has saved all the news items written about them from *The Argus* and *The Bulletin* newspapers.

He said that they joined the Australian Light Horse Brigade when they were twenty years old, but that on their arrival in Gallipoli, they had to become infantrymen because the Turkish cliffs were too steep for their horses. Later on, Mr McGinness became a pilot in Egypt and Mr Fysh became an aircraft observer and machine-gunner. He said they were lucky to have got home alive, as over ten thousand Australian and New Zealand troops were killed over there.

When I told George everything Avery told me, George said anyone who went to war was a hero and bl—y stupid to boot.

13 August 1919—Still Longreach

I have met Mr McGinness. He is twenty-four years old and as tall as Pa, with light brown hair, sticking-out ears and the sharpest blue eyes. I suppose he needs sharp eyes, being a pilot, as he has to look over the side of the aircraft to see where he is going. It must be hard to judge from way up there.

Mr McGinness was wearing his air force uniform with his Distinguished Flying Cross and

Distinguished Conduct Medal, and everyone cheered when he came into the workshop. The owner's daughter called him 'dashing'.

Mr McGinness said George and I must call him 'Ginty' like all his flying pals do. But George said, if he didn't mind, we'd stick to 'Mister', especially as Mr McGinness, being the senior officer, is the boss of our expedition.

Later on, George told me that Mr McGinness was gentry and that Mr Fysh had been educated at a posh Victorian grammar school and brought up with a cook, housemaid, gardener, coachman and nurse. They were squatter class and we were not, he said, and we must never forget it.

After we were introduced, Mr McGinness began talking to George and the boss mechanic, who were working on an automobile next to the one I was polishing. That's how I found out how the survey job came about and what the Defence Department expects of us.

It seems that when Mr McGinness and Mr Fysh arrived home from Egypt after the Great War, they discovered that the Federal Government was offering a 10,000 pound prize for the first Australians to fly from England to Australia in twenty-eight days or less. As Mr Fysh only had a wool-classing job, and Mr McGinness had no job at all, they decided to enter.

The competitors have to be Australian; they have to pay 100 pounds to enter; and they have to supply their own British-made flying machines and make all other necessary arrangements themselves. So, Mr McGinness and Mr Fysh looked up a millionaire bloke called Sir Samuel McCaughey. Sir Samuel had donated a Bristol fighter to No. 1 Squadron of the Australian Flying Corps during the Great War. In fact, Mr McGinness told the boss mechanic that Australians had donated forty-one aircraft to the war effort.

Sir Samuel promised them the money to buy a plane, but he died before he handed it over. So, instead, Mr McGinness and Mr Fysh have taken the job of surveying the air race route, looking for places to build airstrips for the competitors so they can land, refuel, eat, sleep and carry out repairs.

But as Mr Fysh's and Mr McGinness's expertise is aircraft and not automobiles, they need a good automobile mechanic to make sure their Model T Ford finishes the journey. That's where George and I come in.

The boss mechanic slapped George on the back and said there was none better. George only grunted, but I could see a proud gleam in his eye.

Mr McGinness then explained that we would be driving across an area the size of Tasmania (when I got back to the hostel I looked it up in the atlas; it's a long way, Matt). He said we would be following a route chosen by the Defence Department and that it would be the first time an automobile has attempted this route.

I must finish now. Mrs Banks doesn't let us keep the lamp turned up for long; she says it wastes kerosene. And the boys are staging a boxing match in the living room. They are pretending to be Les Darcy, the Australian middleweight champion, fighting the United States champion.

I am getting good at boxing, although last night Avery hit me so hard my nose bled all over the carpet. Halfway through my washing it off, Mrs Banks came in and demanded to know what had happened. I said I had bumped my nose. Well it was a bump. I should have dodged faster. She told me to put ice on it and to leave the carpet.

Mrs Banks and the other Methodist Mission ladies are very kind, even if they insist we go to church three times on Sunday, but I miss you, Mama and Pa. Please don't tell Mama about the boxing. You know how she is about such sports.

Posting this today.

Love, Jack.

15 August 1919—Longreach Motors workshop

Dear Matt,

I received all your letters yesterday but didn't have time to write until today. It was wonderful to hear from you. I am sorry Mrs Wentworth docked your wages over you digging near her prize wisteria plant. How can she imagine that you were trying to kill it? Why didn't she believe you when you told her I had buried a present there for you? What has red hair got to do with dishonesty? And when will she hand over the wrench?

The weather up here is not as hot as I expected, although George says it will be soon. He says in summer I will sleep with only a sheet and a mosquito net.

The workshop's walls and roof are made of corrugated iron, with panes of glass set in the ceiling to let in the daylight. When the sun beats down, George says, it's hotter than the devil's oven. So it will be off with our shirts, and we will all work in singlets and braces, unless a lady comes into the front office. There are quite a few women drivers up here.

Now to answer your questions. The Longreach Motor Company's showroom and workshop are built on the corner of Pelican and Galah Streets (all the streets in Longreach are named after native birds). Above the verandas are two signs saying:

'Longreach Motor Company Limited 1911.

Business. Honest Business. But Business.'

The building has a flagpole, with the Union Jack and the Australian flag flying from it, a horse rail, and a ditch outside, which is the gutter because the roads flood in the summer. Although I can't see how. The land is as flat as a breadboard for as far as the eye can see.

The interior of the workshop is an Aladdin's cave of tools. Pa would be so happy working here.

Under a notice that says, 'We will see that no-one distracts the attention of our men while on your job', is a workspace large enough to assemble twenty or more automobiles. Most are assembled according to the Ford Motor Company's plans, but some are changed, depending on what their owners want.

George says that when someone buys a Model T Ford it's as naked as a baby. This is until the owner adds an assortment of decorative vases, a tartan rug, a rear safety reflector, a fanbelt guide, a clamp-on dash light for reading maps at night, a speedometer, a tool box bolted to the running board, a sun visor, a rear-view mirror, and perhaps a wooden tray in place of the back seat, for carrying sheep.

One farmer wants wide greenhide belts made for his automobile. He wants to pass them under his vehicle's front and rear mudguards to turn it into a tank so he can cross sand. The baker wants a huge box built on his chassis so he can carry his bakery goods inside, out of the way of flies and dust. Mr McGinness's and Mr Fysh's Model T Ford has been turned into a truck.

George has replaced the back seat with a wooden platform, shaded by a canvas hood. It is on this platform and along the running boards and mudguards that our supplies will be stacked, and where George and I will ride. George says we will be sitting on top of each other.

Since my arrival, the adult mechanics have spent most of their time teasing or testing me. They were surprised at how much I knew, and how I didn't fall for their tricks of looking for a left-handed hammer or a pair of left-handed pliers. I told them my father was a train mechanic and that he'd taught me and my twin everything he knew. I didn't say you were a girl. I have a plan.

I forgot to mention that the locals of Longreach are sceptical of us making it to Katherine. They are laying bets in all the pubs as to when the Model T Ford will conk out. Avery said he would bet me a shilling but I said I didn't gamble. The truth is, any shillings I have after I have replaced my cap with a cabbage-tree hat and fly net, I shall send home to Mama and Pa.

Later

I have met Mr Fysh. He is taller and thinner than Mr McGinness, with brown hair, parted in the middle, and very determined brown eyes.

He wore his Flying Corps uniform and Distinguished Flying Cross to the workshop, and all the mechanics cheered. He gave a speech about how, after riding in his first automobile at the age of five, he'd become terrified of them. Of course he was joking, but it made them laugh.

He told everyone that he had just read in the newspaper that two Frenchmen, Lieutenant Poulet and his partner, Benoist, were preparing to enter the air race for the glory of winning, not for the money. Everyone was most indignant, as the race is only for Australians.

Kiss Mama for me on your afternoon off and tell Pa that crutches are very good for killing cockroaches, of which, as you know, our kitchen has battalions.

Love, Jack.

16 August 1919—Cominos Cafe

Dear Matt,

This morning Mr Fysh gave me a list to check that everything we needed was attached to the 'Old Tin Lizzie', which is what he calls the Model T Ford. I'm sure he does this to annoy George, who spends all his time fiddling with the Model T Ford's engine, wheels and tyres, and polishing its black Japanese enamel duco.

George pays him back by saying that anyone who wants to spend their life up in the air must be crackers.

Mr McGinness laughs at both of them and calls us all crackers for trying to cross the top of Australia in a machine that can't fly.

This is what we have loaded in and onto the Tin Lizzie: box Brownie camera, cinemagraphic camera, recording machine, drafting tools for map making, watercolour paints and drawing paper, all for the records Mr Fysh must keep for the Defence Department. Over one mudguard is a suitcase and a tin trunk containing axes, shovels, chains for the wheels and spare inner tubes. Over the other are cans of Mobiloil and eight spare tyres (Goodyear cord because they last 12,000 miles per tyre). In the back, on George's side, are our swags and parcels of knives, rolls of calico, dark and light

Havelock tobacco and Bells matches to exchange for food with the blacks, ammunition, a cast-iron kettle and frying pan, canvas waterbags, and tin cups and plates. On my side are sacks of Feather self-raising flour, Uncle Toby's oats, white sugar, sea salt, black pepper, baking powder, dried milk, custard powder, tea, dried potatoes, jam, golden syrup, peas, beans, Velvet soap, Insectiban fly killer, oil-cloth tarpaulins, a hessian-sided meat safe and a crate of Nestle's condensed milk.

We will keep the meat safe cool by pouring water over the hessian. The condensed milk is in case we get a broken petrol pipe; we can wrap a bit of rag soaked in condensed milk around it. The milk will cement and, as petrol cannot dissolve condensed milk, the pipe will not leak.

Mr McGinness has calculated that we have 1,360 miles to cover to reach Katherine. He has also calculated that Lizzie should be able to do 50 miles a day, making it a twenty-seven day journey. Mr Fysh says we will navigate our way by a compass and the stars, especially the Southern Cross, as there are no roads. He asked me if I knew where magnetic north was. I said I did. Then he sent me down to Cominos to fetch more sugar and twists of tobacco to trade with the blacks for game.

Cominos stocks everything—scent, confectionary, cigars, pipes, cigarettes, Christmas cakes, plum puddings, ham, fruit and toilet creams. It is the most popular cafe and shop in Longreach, but George refuses to buy a pin there. This is because there is a barrier down the middle, dividing the linen-covered tables of the upper-class station owners from the linoleum-covered tables of the hoi polloi. (Do you like my new word? It means the masses, the rabble, workers, us.)

As I know Pa would agree with George, I do not spend my money there either.

17 August 1919—Longreach town

One day before we leave and I still haven't described Longreach.

Imagine a square grid of roads on ground so flat the horizon seems to curve. The roads are wide to enable the drovers to drive their mobs of cattle through the town. Along the roads are boree trees, leopardwood trees (leopardwood seeds can live underground for eight years), bottle trees that contain water in a drought, and acacia trees which are what we call wattle trees and what Mama calls mimosa.

George says there are over five thousand types of acacia, and that they make the best fence posts, as they last in the ground for hundreds of years.

George used to do post and rail fencing before he became a shearer, which was before he became a mechanic.

Longreach is a prosperous town because of the Thomson River and the sheep stations around it. It has fourteen hotels, one on almost every corner, a street of shops, and about a hundred houses. Further out are cattle stations so large it takes weeks to ride a horse over them.

Then there is the hill where Captain Starlight the highwayman watched for the police. The story of Captain Starlight is based on Harry Redford who wasn't a highwayman at all. He was a cattle rustler who stole one thousand head of cattle and drove them from Queensland to South Australia. But it is still a ghostly place. George took me out there on the back of his motorbike after work one afternoon. It was a bumpy ride, as it is only a track. When we got there, it wasn't difficult to imagine the ghost of Captain Starlight hiding amongst the shadows.

Avery has stolen the kerosene lamp. He says the moths that are flocking to it in the hundreds are driving him crazy. He also says I write too much. Avery can hardly read or write, as he left school at nine years old. I said I'd teach him and he punched me. I think that means yes. I'm so glad Mama and Pa taught us.

Posting this with my last tuppeny stamp. I am

also including a list of towns where you can write to me care of the post office. Please write.

Love, Jack.

18 August 1919—Setting off

Dear Matt,

On our way at last. Mr Fysh said it was about time too, but George argued that there was no point in heading off into the blue with an automobile that wasn't fitted out right. He thinks Mr McGinness and Mr Fysh are too cocky and too flaming young. But I reckon if you've been to war, flown flying machines and shot guns at other flying machines, and seen almost eight thousand of your mates die, then you can't be too young for anything.

Before driving off we were photographed with the mechanics of Longreach Motor Company outside the workshop. Then Mr Fysh filmed us with his cinemagraphic camera, with all the Model T Fords parked outside the showroom especially for our send-off.

George wore his best jacket and a straw boater. Mr McGinness wore his summer uniform with a tiger-hunter's pith helmet and Mr Fysh wore his pilot's uniform with a digger's hat. I wore my best trousers, braces and shirt.

As we crossed the Thomson River, Mr Fysh shouted, 'There goes our last bridge and our last yellow perch dinner.'

But Mr McGinness said that there were plenty of fish up north in the Gulf of Carpentaria.

'If ya can catch 'em before the crocs catch you,' grunted George.

Later

We travelled north-west for about 100 miles, with only one inner tube puncture and only once becoming bogged in a dry creek. Mr McGinness said at this rate, we would be there much earlier than he predicted.

George was soaking the tube in a dish of water to find the leak. Mr McGinness and Mr Fysh were off hunting game with their rifles, and I was looking for kindling to start a fire to boil the billy, when I got the fright of my life.

Up from the long grass jumped a half-dressed black man. He was carrying two barbed spears and a long pointed stick, and he had six broad scars carved into his chest. I swear my heart stopped beating I was so scared. Especially as I'd been warned to look out for Murdering Tommy, a black who has killed some settlers and is still at large.

He handed me a speared wallaby and politely asked me if he could have a cuppa in exchange. So I took him back to George, who greeted him with a slap on the back. He then introduced him to me as Lord Billy, a mate he'd met years ago when he was shearing. Adding that Lord Billy was a bonzer cricketer, if he wasn't on walkabout in the bush looking for opal-stone and fossilised bones, which he sold to make his bacca (tobacco) money.

I asked Lord Billy where the bones came from. He told me that long, long ago in the Dreamtime, huge animals ruled the land, only the bush wasn't bush then, it was forests of pine and ferns, and marshlands surrounded an enormous inland sea that reached all the way to the Nullarbor.

I was dubious about this. How could this land, which is as dry as the inside of a kangaroo's pouch, have been an inland sea? George gave me a wink to show that he didn't believe it either. So I asked Lord Billy how big the animals had been.

'Bigger than a house,' he said. 'Some with spears all over him body like echidna and tail so long him brain forget what him tail is doin'. Some like giant flesh-eatin' goannas, some like tree-climbin' possums as big as cows. Plenty big fellas, I'm tellin' you.'

'How do you know what they looked like?' I questioned.

'Long, long time ago, my people find the bones where the big animals die and they draw pictures of the bones on the walls of their caves and in their sand pictures that tell the tribes our Dreamtime stories.'

When Mr McGinness and Mr Fysh came back with two wallabies, I asked them if what Lord Billy had said was true.

Mr McGinness said it was; that ninety-three million years ago there were giant ant-eating ostriches called *Ornithopods* and huge flesh-eating lizards called *Theropods,* gigantic *Titanosaurids* and featherless birds with teeth and wingspans wider than two men's outstretched arms roaming about the land. But they had died millions of years ago.

I asked Mr McGinness how he knew about them, especially their long names.

He said he had studied them as a boy, when an American friend of his father's had come to Australia to look for fossils. He'd become so interested in the subject, he'd got the idea into his head that he would become a palaeontologist, which is someone who searches for fossils. But his father told him that it was a rich man's hobby and that there was no money in it, so Mr McGinness gave up the idea.

George said, 'Well I never.' But I know he didn't

believe Mr McGinness any more than he believes Lord Billy.

When we set off, Lord Billy came too. Balancing on the footboard and hanging onto the edge of the windscreen, he pointed out all the birds and named them for me. There were wedge-tailed eagles, Major Mitchell cockatoos, brown larks, sand martins, desert chats no bigger than grasshoppers, and my favourites, tiny blue waxbills with yellow bills and yellow feet as thin as cotton thread.

That evening when we reached Winton, the main street was a swirling dust bowl. It was hard to believe Mr Fysh when he said last summer he'd seen an automobile bogged to its front axle in mud in the middle of it.

Mr Fysh and Mr McGinness booked into the North Gregory Hotel, George and I put our tent up beside Lizzie, as we are now calling her, and Lord Billy left to visit some friends who live on the edge of town.

After he'd gone, George told me that although Lord Billy's family lived in a shantytown near Longreach, they weren't from Longreach, because the Iningai tribe, who had once lived there, had died out in the 1902 drought. Lord Billy wasn't from Winton either, because the Kia tribe of the Winton district had been killed off by the early settlers.

Later

I'm writing by the light from the hotel window.

Winton, which was once called Pelican Waterhole, is where the next airstrip after Longreach will be built. Mr Fysh and Mr McGinness have already decided where to put it.

This evening, George took me to Winton's Royal Theatre as a treat, because he said I was turning out to be a good sport.

The Royal Theatre is an open-air theatre with rows of deckchairs. We saw a film called *Kids' Stakes* with Fatty Fynn in it.

I told him that Sydney has 150 open-air cinemas, but with hard benches, not deckchairs, and that in the city's theatre palaces, there were female attendants in long velvet dresses with torches to show you to your padded seat.

He said it was hard to believe. I don't think George believes me any more than he believes Lord Billy's or Mr McGinness's big animals.

19 August 1919—Winton

This morning, just before dawn, I woke up to scratching on the canvas tent. Then I heard Lord Billy whisper that if I was quick, he'd show me something very important. George said I could go, as long as I was back before Mr Fysh and Mr McGinness finished breakfast.

It was a long trek and still dark. Lord Billy didn't make any noise as we jogged through the silvery Mitchell grass. I wish I could move like that. I sounded like an elephant running behind him.

This time he wasn't carrying his spears, just his long pointed stick which he uses to dig up the big animals' bones. As the sun was turning the distant jagged edge of the Tully Ranges scarlet, and the birds' chorus was becoming so loud I had to cover my ears, we reached a waterhole. Lord Billy described it as, 'Him little fella now, but when rain come, him big fella, and in Dreamtime, him big sea.'

Silently and bent double, Lord Billy crept towards the water so as not to disturb the ducks, magpie geese, green parrots and pink-beaked pelicans feeding there. I followed, not as silently, but holding my breath.

With one foot suspended, Lord Billy stopped, pointed, and there they were. Hundreds of big animal footprints embedded in what, he whispered, had once been a slick of mud before it turned to rock. There were medium-size three-toed prints, little claw prints, and huge round-toed prints, a leap apart.

'This big fella chase this little fella. This little

fella plenty scared. Wheel round here, here, here. Big fella catch plenty little fella,' he explained.

Carefully placing his feet on one print and then another, he acted out how the smaller of the big animals had cowered and trembled, then whirled and fled, while the giant animals roared, reared up, advanced, attacked and killed.

When he roared, all the birds on the lake took flight, forming a rainbow arc over our heads.

Then he crouched down, stroking the prints the way we would stroke a cat. 'All gone now,' he sighed. 'Even great, great, grandfather emu bird that swallow up stones to grind up the plants him fill him belly with.'

He looked so sad, Matt. As if someone in his family had died. Then he grinned at me through his whiskers and whispered, 'But sometimes him come back. Lord Billy see him, hear him. Come back night time. Him called Minumpi with tin roof on him back and big triangle head. Him with bird feet up Diamantina River way. Him big like train carriage, big enough to fight giant crocodile, big enough to eat ten blackfellas in one bite. You listen, you hear him too.'

He lay down and put his ear to the footprints. I did the same, and Matt, honestly, I heard them. I heard the *thump, thump, thump* of their huge feet and their strange bellowing to each other.

As soon as I nodded that I'd heard, Lord Billy jumped up and put his ear to a nearby lark salmon gum. I did the same and I swear I heard hoarse squawks and high-pitched squeaks coming from high up. Then, when I looked up into the tree's branches, I saw (well, I thought I saw) a huge nest, with enormous baby birds with teeth-filled beaks fighting each other for the food their giant leather-winged parent was feeding them.

'Now we run back quick before min min light or mama bird catch us,' shouted Lord Billy, breaking the spell and taking off without waiting for me.

We sprinted all the way and arrived just in time. George had packed our tent and swags. Mr Fysh had photographed the place where he thought an airstrip should be built, if this route was accepted, and Mr McGinness was already in the driving seat.

Lord Billy didn't come with us. The last I saw of him was his torn trousers flapping around his ankles, his toes covered in dust, and his old felt hat pulled down so far I could only see his grey beard.

'So where did he take you?' asked George.

'To see some big animal footprints,' I told him.

George laughed. 'You don't want to believe everything you see when you're with Lord Billy.'

'What do you mean?' I demanded.

But then I remembered the giant leather-winged birds perched on the edge of their nest, feeding their chicks, and as I know there are no such things, I decided not to mention them.

Instead, I asked George what a min min light was. He said it was a ghost that early settlers and prospectors swore they had seen; that they were round white lights that followed you, and if they caught you then . . .

'Then what?' I asked.

He laughed and poked me in the stomach. 'How do I know? I've never seen one.'

He asked me if I'd noticed how Lord Billy had held his spear in his left hand with the tip towards us.

'That's to show he is friendly. If he'd held it butt end towards us, it would mean he was preparing to attack. A black swings his spear from left to right across his body, butt end first, to fit into his woomera or throwing stick, which is held in his right hand. Back goes his right arm and he throws. He can do this as fast or faster than a settler can aim and fire his gun.'

George has great admiration for the blacks. He says they make wonderful stockmen and some of the best shearers and drovers he'd ever met, especially the women who, dressed in men's clothing, worked harder and faster than most white drovers.

20 August 1919—Somewhere north of Winton

I hurt all over. Lizzie is a boneshaker. But the worst thing is her gravity fuel system.

A Model T Ford's petrol tank is above the engine in front of the driver, with a vertical glass tube coming through the dashboard so he can see how much fuel there is.

Normally, the fuel flows down to the carburettor, but the minute Lizzie goes up a hill it flows backwards, making the engine splutter and stop. Then, if the driver doesn't heave on the handbrake, she rolls backwards, usually into a creek bed, which means I have to crank the crank handle again.

Cranking is dangerous because the crank handle can jerk back and bash me in the hand, arm or shoulder. It has become clear to me that Lizzie will start only when Lizzie wants to. So, to trick her, I have to pretend I am not interested in her starting, then, when the driver turns on the ignition, I crank the crank handle fast to start her before she knows what I am doing. When she starts it is with a few loud bangs and an ear-splitting explosion, and if the handbrake has been released, she does a little bounce forward, forcing me to leap out of the way or I'd be run over.

Mr McGinness has a new way of getting Lizzie to start off faster. He pulls down hard on a lever attached to the steering column while at the same time stamping down on the low-speed pedal. Lizzie lunges forward with a roar like a chained lion. Mr McGinness takes his foot off the brake pedal, Lizzie catapults into top gear and we are away.

Only we weren't on our way today. Lizzie catapulted upwards and rolled backwards at least ten times. Twice she almost ran over George, Mr Fysh and myself. We were pushing from behind. We don't do that any more.

George suggested we pump air into the tank with a bicycle pump that he has modified for that purpose. Mr McGinness said backing up would work as well, and that everyone in Melbourne backs up hills.

Can you imagine it, Matt? All those city motor cars going uphill backwards. It must be a funny sight. I have added Melbourne to my list of places to visit.

During the day, we built three dirt ramps down into three dry creek beds and three dirt ramps out again. We laced the sand with saplings and long grass so Lizzie's narrow tyres wouldn't slip, and we put chains on them so they'd grip. But at the third creek, part of the ramp gave way and Lizzie almost toppled over onto Mr Fysh, who had fallen off the edge.

George and I pushed extra hard and Lizzie made it. Mr Fysh said we'd saved his life.

21 August 1919—Somewhere south of Kynuna

I'm up early to light the fire and fill the billy from our canvas waterbags as there is no water nearby.

The dawn birds are a wonder. There are rainbow twits, red-beaked and -cheeked zebra finches, pink- and yellow-crested cockatiels, magpie larks, and whistling kites. Fortunately they are all too small to be worth hunting by Mr Fysh or Mr McGinness, as I think they are too pretty to eat.

Behind me I can hear a rustling in the fallen bark. It could be dingoes or wallabies, or Lord Billy's giant snakes, or his huge one-toed, carnivorous kangaroo.

George has woken up. He says there were dingoes sniffing around last night; they must have smelt the leftover rabbit stew in the meat safe. Fortunately the meat safe was hanging high on a tree branch.

Yesterday George taught me how to skin and gut a rabbit. It is the smelliest, most revolting thing

I have ever done. No wonder Mama prefers the rabbito to do it. When we threw the guts away, I saw a huge wedge-tailed eagle hovering overhead, but George said they prefer their prey to be alive. He said the dingoes will eat the guts.

Later

We finally reached Kynuna. We sang *Waltzing Matilda* as we drove into the small town, as it is near here, at the Combo Waterhole, that Banjo Patterson wrote *Waltzing Matilda*. Also near here is Dagwood Cattle Station, where a young lady called Miss Christina Macpherson put his words to a popular Scottish tune.

George says Banjo Patterson was crazy to have sold the tune for only a five guinea coin, just to see it printed on the outside of a Billy Tea tin. He also says that Banjo Patterson was a city solicitor and a war correspondent. I always thought Banjo Patterson was a swaggie.

Kynuna has three iron and tin windmills, three iron and tin hotels, a billiard saloon, a match factory, a cordial works, a bush hospital (with no sick people inside, because I peeked), a Cobb and Co depot next door to the blacksmith's shop, and a corrugated-iron post office and telegraph station.

While the men went to wet their whistle in the

billiard saloon, I went to the post office, where I am now, addressing this letter to send to you.

Love, Jack.

Later—Outside Selwyn

Dear Matt,

The Kynuna post office lady was pleased to take my letters and pleased to have a chat. She has a hard job. She is the postmistress, the telegraph operator, the telephone exchange operator, and the agent for Cobb and Co coaches.

She sells stamps, sorts letters, and sends telegraphs by morse code, which is a lot of dots and dashes sent over a radio, allowing people to send messages from anywhere to anywhere in minutes. She sells coach tickets, collects and sends mail, cooks for passengers going through if they don't want to go to the hotel, looks after the ladies, changes the horses for fresh ones, and waters and feeds the tired horses. It was a wonder she had time for a chat.

Her most interesting parcels have been a box of chickens to water and feed, a basket of kittens to give milk to, and a baby.

I said a baby was a passenger not a parcel.

She disagreed. She said it was a parcel, as it was unaccompanied, due to its mother having died, and it was being 'posted' to its grandparents in the next town.

After I explored Kynuna, which took five minutes, I waited for the men on the pub steps. Here I was joined by a real old-timer called Mr Chick McLaren; he said Chick was short for Charles.

Mr McLaren was wearing the greasiest waistcoat I have ever seen, and baggy trousers tied around the waist with rope and around the knees with string, to protect his legs from snakes and spiders. On his matted hair, he wore a shapeless digger's hat that had been his grandson's, before his grandson was killed in France during the Great War. It was kept on with string tied under his white whiskers.

'Never take it off,' he said. 'Not waking nor sleeping. Never know when I might have company and a hat is the sign of a gentleman.'

He said he'd been born in Halls Creek in 1830 and had walked all over Australia. He said Kynuna was perfect for opals, as they were made from water dripping through the black soil and sticking in the sandstone, and Kynuna had plenty of black soil and sandstone.

I asked if he'd found any opals.

He said he hadn't, so he'd gone digging for gold in Pumpkin Gully where the largest nugget in Queensland had been found.

So I asked if he had found any gold.

He said not yet, so he was heading north-east where there were a lot of ironstone, quartz and copper deposits. If he didn't find gold there, he'd head for Georgetown, where blind Freddy could pick up a fistful of sapphires, garnets, and topaz just for the looking.

Then I asked him if he'd seen any animal bones or footprints, big animals the size of houses. He shook his head and said, 'You've been out in the sun too long, laddie.'

Then his dark blue eyes lit up like beacons, and he asked me if I wanted to come waltzing matilda with him. He said that prospecting was a good life and I would never regret it. It was the fastest way to becoming rich. Ridgy-didge, Bluey!

'Ridgy-didge' is the way people up here say truly, or really, or honestly. 'Bluey' is what they call redheads.

I explained that I wanted to be a mechanic and own my own garage, but I thanked him for his offer.

At this he took hold of my hand with his dirt-encrusted fingers and drew a line down the middle of my palm.

'This is your gold line,' he said. 'It's as strong as a railroad track. You'll find gold or something close to it. Mark my words. Ridgy-didge, Bluey my boy!'

So you see, Matt, we will get our garage one day.

Then I made the mistake of saying that he and I had the same surname and might be related. He shook his head fast and said how there was a mob of McLarens in Australia, none of them related. After that he didn't speak to me again.

When Mr Fysh, Mr McGinness and George came out of the pub, Mr McLaren asked for a lift to McKinlay, where he had a mate. So they squashed him, his swag, walking stick, soot-encrusted billy, tin cup and miner's pick, in between George and me.

Just before we reached McKinlay, the landscape became very hilly with lots of rocky gullies full of gidgee trees. Mr McLaren said he could smell gold and asked to be let off, so Mr Fysh stopped and the old-timer climbed off.

After we'd driven away, Mr Fysh said he was glad to see the back of the old codger as he'd had enough of his ravings about Lasseter's gold and enough of his smell.

He did stink something terrible, Matt. I don't think he had bathed for years, but I liked him. I wonder if we are related? I wonder if Pa has any uncles called Chick?

I asked George who Lasseter was. He said that around 1897 a prospector called Harry Lasseter found a reef of gold as tall as himself, but that nobody else knew where it was. George said he didn't believe the reef existed. He also said that gold fever was catching and that Chick McLaren had it something bad.

After McKinlay, the land became very rough until we drove through Selwyn, another mining town of shadeless tin houses and tents jammed between eroded red hills.

During the Great War, Selwyn's Mt Elliott copper mine produced a world record 30,000 tons of copper. People from every state flocked to work there. It became a boom town. But with the war over, there was no need for copper, so the mine closed down and the people disappeared.

George waved at the empty pitheads. 'Four years of fame. Now only min min lights, ghosts of miners, and bushfires lit by the blacks to regenerate the bush in the hope that it will grow over the pit scars.'

So far, Matt, we have been following drovers' tracks, so we haven't had to chop our way through scrub, but we have been bogged in more creeks than I can remember.

Although the creeks are bone dry at the moment, during the wet, they become raging torrents. Which is why the government doesn't bother to build bridges or railway lines over them, because they would be washed away each summer.

Mr McGinness knew of a bridge that was washed away with a buggy still on it. The bridge, buggy, and the three young ladies who were coming to play tennis with him, ended up 50 miles downstream.

He says when the rains come, the black soil turns into a quagmire and clings to everything: boots, hoofs, wagon- and coach-wheels, and automobile tyres. That's why he is sure that his and Mr Fysh's idea of an aerial service connecting the railheads of Charleville, Longreach, Winton and Cloncurry with Katherine and Darwin, is a good one.

He says they already have such services in Europe and Britain and that Australia is lagging behind. He says this is why he and Mr Fysh are so keen to map out where the airstrips between Longreach and Darwin will go, because in the long run, their aerial service will be using them. 'Killing one bird with two stones,' he calls it.

George says the reason Mr Fysh and Mr McGinness are so keen to start an aerial service is that it will give them a job they like to do. He also says the aerial service tickets will be so costly that only the cattle station owners and cattle or sheep buyers will be able to afford them. The likes of us will still have to travel by Cobb and Co to a railhead.

Let me explain about the railheads, Matt. They

are at the ends of the railway lines that come inland from the coast. The drovers take their cattle to the railheads, then the cattle are transported in open rail trucks to the ports of Brisbane, Rockhampton and Townsville and put on ships to go south.

The railway lines do not go all the way across Queensland, as there are not enough white people to fill one compartment, let alone four. All Queensland trains have to have four compartments: a first-class male compartment, a first-class female compartment, a second-class male compartment and a second-class female compartment.

I think George is right about Mr Fysh and Mr McGinness wanting an aerial service so they can fly all the time. It's all they ever talk about.

22 August 1919—Somewhere north-west of Selwyn

So ends another day of bumping Lizzie down into creek beds. Easily enough done once the petrol cans, suitcases and stores are removed by me (George is afraid the Mobiloil cans will explode). But almost impossible to get out of, even driving backwards.

I like being with George. As we bounce along, he tells me all about when he was a shearer. He says he wasn't fast like Jack Howe, who shore a record of 321 sheep in seven hours and forty minutes, but he was a steady worker.

He says one station he'd worked at had over a hundred shearing sheds, all shearing at the same time. He was paid 10 shillings for every hundred sheep sheared. When he describes how, before the railways, wool was carried to the nearest port on wagons drawn by thirty draft horses, wonderful animals with tails that touched the ground and manes as soft as a woman's hair, I can almost see the horses.

George reckons shearing is a smarter game than droving, even if it pays less, because he'd rather have corns on his hands than corns on his rear end from a saddle. He also reckons that shearing is smarter than being a railway worker, as their living conditions are worse than those of the shearers. He says that it was because of the bad living conditions that so many men signed up to go to war, just to get away from them.

He says the graziers still don't provide decent living conditions for the shearers, and that any man, shearer, drover, railway worker or teamster, who has to walk or ride a bicycle from station to station, not knowing if there is a job waiting there or not, or having to work ten hours a day, deserves a better deal than a fly-ridden dunny hole and no flywire screens on their cookhouse. He reckons there's another big shearers' strike coming up.

I told him Bert, the rouseabout I'd met on the train, said the same thing.

This afternoon Mr Fysh drove up and down one creek for two hours looking for a way out, as the banks were so steep. In the end we dug a gigantic slope that took three hours. The next creek was full of mud, so we winched Lizzie through. When we made camp, Mr Fysh said we'd only done 10 miles.

Mr McGinness said not to worry. It had taken him and his horse forty-three days to reach Gallipoli by ship. He also said that out of the 7,843 horses, only 224 had died at sea. Then he told me the saddest thing. He said when the Australians enlisted in the Australian Light Horse Brigade, they had to provide their own horses, but on arriving off Turkey, the British generals told them to off-load the horses down the coast. Later, when they left Gallipoli, rather than let the horses fall into the hands of the enemy, they had to shoot them. Mr McGinness said he cried when he shot his horse.

23 August 1919—Somewhere near Battle Mountain

After a day of bogged wheels, of unpacking Lizzie and repacking her, of making four separate fires to boil the billy to make four lots of tea while George mended tubes, we have finally stopped for the night. We are camped at the crossroads of two major stock routes, beside a billabong. Mr Fysh shot some freckled ducks then swam out to retrieve them. George and I plucked them and salted them, as Mr McGinness had shot a yellow-footed wallaby during the day and it was already baking on the fire.

Wallaby meat is a pleasant change from the salt beef we have been eating since we left Winton. Mr Fysh joked that eating salt beef would save us from being eaten by the blacks. I asked George what Mr Fysh meant. George said that in the late 1800s blacks used to eat the gold prospectors, but they preferred Chinamen, as white people were too salty from eating too much salt beef.

I guess I must have looked scared because he assured me that the tradition of 'eating kidney fat' didn't happen nowadays. Most blacks were law-abiding, at least all the ones he knew, and he knew a fair few.

24 August 1919—Cloncurry

It's night again and we are in Cloncurry, which is another small town of rusting copper furnaces, makeshift huts with corrugated iron, tarpaulin, or melaleuca bark roofs, dirt floors, and the round corrugated water tanks, which are often larger than the shanties they lean against.

Cloncurry was a boom town once.

'And could be again,' said a Schaeffe Street shopkeeper, who tried to sell George and me some picks and shovels to go prospecting for gold and copper in the nearby Selwyn Ranges. 'There are still gougers out there sinking shafts and finding gold,' he said.

'How often?' George asked.

'Now and then,' he grinned.

'Not now and then enough,' laughed George. 'Give me a spanner and an engine any time.'

The shopkeeper told us that it was near here, on the banks of the Corella River, that Burke and Wills, the famous explorers, camped in 1861. Then he tried to sell us some handpainted postcards of the place.

George reckoned it was a foregone conclusion that Burke and Wills would die, because they set off in the wet season and because they needed some local blacks such as Kalkadoons with them;

outsiders would not have been allowed to drink at the local tribes' waterholes without permission. He reckons Mr King, the only one of the party to survive, was lucky to be found by a friendly tribe and nursed back to health.

Cloncurry is where Mr Fysh and Mr McGinness plan to build the third airstrip. This is a big improvement on Cobb and Co coaches. They have to change horses every 25 to 30 miles.

While Mr Fysh took photographs and did some quick watercolour sketches for the Defence Department of where the landing field would be and its surroundings, so it could be identified from the air, Mr McGinness started to do a deal with the locals in the Leichardt Hotel as to who would build it.

Most of those he spoke to didn't believe a flying machine would come anywhere near their town, but they liked the idea of earning some easy government money.

George and I went off to purchase some fencing wire and vegetables. On the way we passed a huge gold prospectors' cemetery full of the graves of hundreds of Chinamen and a few Afghanis.

George said he didn't mind walking past it in daylight but he wouldn't go near it at night; that he wasn't afraid of min min lights, *yun-yis* or Kalkadoon ghosts, but the sword-swinging ghost of a Chinaman was something fearful. I asked if he had ever seen one and he said he hadn't. Then I asked him what a Kalkadoon ghost was.

This is what he told me. In 1884 some settlers built their homestead beside a Kalkadoon waterhole, somewhere close to where we had camped last night (he didn't tell me this last night because he saw how scared I was about being eaten).

When the Kalkadoon came down to fetch water, the settlers shot at them. In retaliation, the Kalkadoon killed the settlers. When other settlers heard of the murders, they sent for help and out came Sub-Inspector Urquhart with his troopers. At a place called Battle Mountain, he and his troops massacred almost the entire Kalkadoon tribe, men, women and children, numbering somewhere around five hundred souls.

George said it was a disgraceful affair, as it was spears against troopers' and settlers' carbines. The waterhole was on Kalkadoon traditional land and they had a right to get angry if they were shot at. When the blacks killed the settlers it was called 'an atrocity', but when the settlers killed blacks it was called 'saving the water for the cattle' or 'reprisal'. Back at our camp I asked Mr Fysh what he thought about the Kalkadoon massacre. His answer was, 'The settlers were opening up the country, so their cattle had priority.'

'The Kalkadoon were here first,' argued George. 'The settlers should have shared the water.'

'The blacks weren't doing anything productive with the land,' replied Mr Fysh.

I thought George would burst at that. 'There isn't a law that says they have to,' he grunted.

'Then there should be,' said Mr Fysh.

It looked like they might argue all night, when Mr McGinness changed the subject by saying how lucky it was that no-one owned the air, because that's where he wanted to be, up in it flying like an eagle. And did I know that at this very moment (because in England it is day when it is night here) there were English pilots flying ten aircraft a day from London to Belgium, delivering food and clothing to the war refugees? And that in South Africa a passenger could fly from Johannesburg to Capetown for only 20 pounds return?

I said I didn't know either of those things and 20 pounds seemed a lot of money to me. But I have put Johannesburg and Capetown on my list of places to go.

What I do know, Matt, is that Australia once belonged to the blacks and now it doesn't. And Mr McGinness said he and Mr Fysh had gone to war to stop the Germans from taking the land that belonged to the French, the Polish and the English. So if the Germans were wrong to want other people's land, weren't the settlers wrong too? And if they were, aren't we all wrong? George says that thinking too much will give me a headache. I wish you were here to talk it over with.

Mr McGinness's change of subject worked and all was going well until he said that it would cost the Defence Department 500 pounds to build the Cloncurry airstrip. He considered this a bit steep considering there were so many out of work miners, brumby catchers and Afghani camel drivers hanging around doing nothing. He thought that maybe they should employ the blacks instead as it would be cheaper.

At that, George stalked off to have a cigarette on his own.

Later, when we were going to bed, I asked George why he had become angry again. He said that he'd just found out that the Australian taxpayer would be paying for our surveying trip and the building of Mr Fysh's and Mr McGinness's landing strips, but that when the flights from London to Australia commenced, the route would be sold to English private enterprise.

'But Mr Fysh and Mr McGinness are going to have their own Australian aerial service,' I argued.

'And shearers will shear kangaroos first,' he grunted.

George is calling for me to turn down the

hurricane lamp and come to bed. I will post this tomorrow.

Love, Jack.

27 August 1919—Gulf of Carpentaria

Dear Matt,

Three easy days. We travelled from the red hills of Cloncurry to the savanna grasslands south of the Gulf of Carpentaria with only one mishap (digging ramps to get out of creek beds is considered a normal day's work, not a mishap). Our mishap happened just before we reached Dobblyn, another Cobb and Co coach stop.

Lizzie became stuck in the mud at the bottom of a river, and she would be there still if a mob of blacks on walkabout from Burketown hadn't come along.

What a jolly lot they were, although scantily dressed to say the least. The women wore no blouses and the men wore no trousers, just torn bits of material around their waists.

Naked or not, George blessed them, because the men put down their spears and fire sticks, and the women, their coolamons and the nets of wriggling frogs they'd collected, and all put their shoulders to Lizzie. They pushed so hard she raced up the river bank putting to flight a flock of grey brolgas.

Mr Fysh gave our saviours four twists of tobacco for their trouble and three pieces of red calico for the women, two of whom had not removed the nets they wore over their shoulders. I could see two babies and a puppy sleeping inside them. The group left singing and laughing and waving back at us. I am sure they were making jokes about us.

George said they were probably on their way to repaint the caves their tribe had been visiting since before the Dreamtime, or on walkabout around their tribal land to retell their myths and legends, which is their way of remembering their history.

'Wherever they're off to,' he told me, 'it's sacred and secret and they'd die first before telling anyone.'

Further on we heard some long drawn-out calls. George said it was the calling language blacks used to keep in touch over long distances. Ten minutes later we passed another mob heading in the same direction as the first. As we passed they shouted, 'Bacca, shoo-gar boss.' But we didn't stop.

Burketown is another four hours drive up the track and we want to arrive before dark.

Later—Burketown

Burketown at last and we arrived before nightfall. No mail for me. Perhaps there will be some brought up from Cloncurry when the weekly mailman rides up.

When we drove into town, with Lizzie limping along with one tyre full of grass, you'd have thought we were celebrities. Mr Fysh and Mr McGinness were wearing their air force uniforms and everyone came out to gawk. George was embarrassed but I felt very important.

Mr McGinness and Mr Fysh went off to the Burketown Hotel with the police sergeant and a Mr Shadford, to discuss where to put an airstrip and how to get supplies in for the air race competitors. Later, Mr Fysh said that when Mr Shadford heard that our next stop would be Borroloola, he scoffed at our over-laden vehicle, saying it would never get there, because no automobile has ever travelled the northern route.

Mr Fysh told Mr Shadford that if he had seen how well the Ford ambulances and Model T Fords of the No. 1 Australian Light Car Patrol had performed in Jordan and around the Dead Sea, he would think differently.

So that's another thing I have to find out. Why is the Dead Sea dead?

28 August 1919—Burketown

Burketown is one of the most isolated towns in Australia. It is 260 miles from Cloncurry and as far north as one can go before falling into the sea. Although, it would be hard to fall into the sea, as one of the locals said that it is rimmed with miles of khaki-green mangrove swamps and swirling black mud full of evil-looking, plate-sized crabs.

There are more hessian-bag dunnies in this town than houses. This is because the town has to be rebuilt every few years due to the voracious eating habits of the local white ants (which are really termites). So some people live in tents.

The three houses, two stores and hotel are on one side of the Albert River while the blacks' camp is on the other. The Albert River is home to saltwater crocodiles twice as long as Lizzie. I haven't seen any, but they worry George.

He says I go around with my eyes shut and he is insisting that I keep them wide open and stop daydreaming, as crocodiles can move as fast as horses and can take down a buffalo and swallow it in one gulp. If this happened to me, what would he tell our mother?

But the owner of the Burketown Hotel told me that crocs don't swallow their victims in one gulp. They roll them under the water to drown them, then stash them away in an underwater cave until their catch is rotten and easy to pull apart. I think I'd rather be swallowed in one gulp.

George and I put up our tent beneath a cabbage palm, a good distance from the river, but as close to Lizzie as possible. We need to make sure that all the people (black, white, yellow and in between) who are milling around touching and poking at everything, don't take anything.

29 August 1919—Burketown again

When I woke up this morning, the tent walls were crowded with frog-mouthed geckos clinging to the canvas and the tent poles. In the bright sun their little green bodies were transparent.

Last night I dreamt of spear-throwing Kalkadoon warriors and sword-wielding, Chinese-screeching ghosts. I woke up shrieking to find that it was already daylight and that my ghost was a cheeky possum who was in the tent ransacking our flour provisions.

George was off buying 47 gallons of petrol and some birdcage netting, Mr Fysh was off taking photographs of where he thought an airstrip should be built, and Mr McGinness was unpacking Lizzie and giving away all our unessential items in an attempt to lighten her.

Within half an hour, our tents, spare clothing and extra pots and pans were gone. I am sure this diary would have gone too if I hadn't kept it with me.

Mr Fysh returned with a new map drawn by an old-timer called Mr Smith. He said we would be following the tracks of the German explorer Leichhardt who went this way in 1845.

I told him that the Sydney suburb I lived in was named after Leichhardt, and he promised if we got to Katherine in one piece, he would add 5 pounds to my wages because of it.

He's a funny cove. Serious most of the time, always methodical and meticulous, especially with the Defence Department's paperwork, maps and photographs; whereas Mr McGinness, who is the leader of our survey team, is noisy and funny and not a bit meticulous about anything.

George told Mr McGinness that he drives Lizzie as if he is up in the sky with nothing to bump into but clouds, which is why he bumps into everything on the track. Mr McGinness joked back that George treated Lizzie as if she were a living, breathing human being. But then he added that he understood that because he treated his aircraft in exactly the same way. I understand both of them, because it's the same way Pa used to treat his trains.

Mr Fysh thinks that as we will be driving through an area populated with unbranded cleanskins (cattle), which we can legally shoot, we'll be able to provide food for ourselves. But we have to take care, as there are gangs of cattleduffers hiding in the hills. Not to mention tons of sand to bog us down, and plenty of running rivers and creeks to block our way.

'As if we haven't had enough of those already,' grunted George.

I hope we meet a cattleduffer.

Later

This afternoon, the Albert River steamer arrived bringing out-of-date letters to me from you and Mama. It will take my letters to you when it leaves. I have been assured by the postmaster they will reach you faster.

The steamer comes from Rockhampton. It travels north around the top of Cape of York, through Torres Strait, along the coast of the Gulf of Carpentaria, until it reaches the Albert River, where it chugs 20 miles south through the mangrove swamps. As it approaches Burketown with its deck piled high with cargo, hidden but not protected under salt-encrusted tarpaulins, it sounds its horn and everyone comes running.

One of the out-of-town settlers, a bow-legged man clearly more used to the saddle than walking, told me that the steamer's cargo was usually salt-damaged, going rusty, or full of maggots. The sugar and tea casks were more often than not cracked or broken, with the sugar inside gone black and sticky and the tea tasting like mouldy gum leaves.

Even so, he said, he was glad that it had arrived at last. He had ordered a Singer sewing machine for his wife and a new saddle for himself and he'd been waiting for them for four months. He also wanted to read the newspapers and catch up with the news.

George said the newspapers were so old, a war could have been started and won before this man read about it.

Everyone cheered as the steamer pulled in beneath the melaleuca trees. Not only were they glad to get their letters and goods, but the hotel owner had promised them a dance once he'd unloaded his stock of Macs beer. The dance will be tomorrow night.

Now to your letters. I am glad you have found so much literature on aviation and that you find it so interesting.

How strange to think of you learning how to set a table with that many knives, forks and spoons while all the time you are thinking about propellers and engines. Why do they need so much cutlery? I bet they wouldn't use as much if they had to wash it all.

How does Mrs Wentworth expect you to clean the family's and guests' shoes and not have nugget under your fingernails?

Don't worry, Matt, it is not forever, my plan will save you.

Isn't it good news about Pa being able to walk with a stick? Give them my love.

Love, Jack.

31 August 1919—The Burketown dance

Dear Matt,

What an exciting day yesterday was—too exciting for me to sit down and write until now. First there was Curly, the self-appointed town crier, strolling around all day, ringing his bell and shouting through his ginger beard about all that was to take place, and that there are fresh oranges for sale at tuppence an orange.

People began getting ready for the festivities first thing in the morning. Men took baths in galvanised bath tubs, set up close enough to the river to make filling them easy, but not close enough to be eaten by a stray croc. Others, braces down and shirts off, had their hair and moustach trimmed by their mates or wives.

Boys groomed their goats and spit-and-polished their carts. On the hotel veranda, the town bookie, Mr Clarence, who is also the town shopkeeper, sold oranges and took bets on all the activities. Children ran wild everywhere, shrieking and screaming, and dragging their soapbox carts behind them, although Burketown is as flat as an ironing table.

Blacks came in from their camps dressed in a strange assortment of kangaroo skins and whitefella's cast-offs. The women were given a bolt of calico by the hotel owner's wife who said she wanted them to be decently covered and not turning up bare-breasted in coconut-fibre skirts.

Even Mr Yuan, the market gardener, came to town with his tiny little wife who looks more like a doll tottering along on her teeny feet than a real person. The storekeeper said Mr Yuan ordered her from Hong Kong just the way we would order a suit from a catalogue, and the way Ali Baba the Afghan cameleer ordered his wife. I wonder if she got a shock when she saw Burketown.

Here is a list of the activities that took place.

At 2 pm a baby weight-guessing competition. At 2.30 pm a boys wrestling competition. At 3 pm a goat cart derby. At 3.30 pm the tricycle and

. At 4 pm a girls-only skipping race. At
egatta on the river (blacks canoeing
ıck). At 5 pm a boxing match in the
main street. At 7 pm the dance.

The billygoat cart races were bonzer fun. I got to participate because a boy I wrestled and beat declared me to be his best mate. I am ashamed to say our little cart, pulled by one billygoat, was beaten by a cart carrying two women, pulled by three nanny-goats. But only because our left wheel fell off and we were tipped into the dust. The billygoat was so surprised that it peed a waterfall of pee a hand's span from our faces.

George said I was lucky not to land face down in goat poo, as there was plenty of it around. George was in a good mood because he'd guessed the weight of a baby and won two bottles of beer, and he'd put a bet on me winning the wrestling match (although he insisted he was not a betting man) and he'd won a pound.

After the goat cart races came the three-wheel and two-wheel bike races. Some of the tricycles were so rusty, with makeshift seats and odd-sized pedals, that I was amazed they could be ridden. A black boy, whose legs kept hitting the handlebars, won.

The two-wheeler bikes were all men's bicycles, ridden by boys with their right leg stuck under the bar, because they were too small to sit on the seats and reach the pedals. My new best mate, Snowy, won one of the races, so we celebrated by sharing a thruppenny bottle of lemonade.

To get ready for the dance, I polished my shoes, for what it is worth in this dusty place. My shirt was unironed but clean, and my best trousers had been pressed under a board all day. I slicked down my hair with Brylcreem so it would not curl and would look darker; red hair not being favoured by girls, or so said my new best mate. His hair is bleached white by the sun and, by the way the girls cheered his bicycle ride, I think blond hair must be very popular.

The dance was held in a ramshackle hall attached to the hotel. The entire town came, as well as a mob of gold and copper miners, some drovers with their skinny, leather-faced wives and skinnier children, some prosperous-looking cattle agents, and the local graziers with their families, who are very lah-di-dah.

The music was provided by Miss Betty, the school teacher, who played a piano with lopsided brass candelabras attached at each end. Mr Clarence played the accordion.

A lot of the time Miss Betty, who is pretty and single and, George says, 'Looking for a bloke', was away dancing, as there was a shortage of female partners. This shortage didn't stop the men from dancing. They waltzed together, stiffly at first, then very grandly as they drunk more beer, then wildly as they became drunker.

Everyone was wearing their best clothes, mine for the last time, as they were given away this morning. The men wore shirts (with detachable collars), ties, jackets and wide-brimmed hats that they took off as soon as they entered the hall. Mr McGinness and Mr Fysh wore their dress uniforms and black lace-up pumps. Most of the boys wore trousers or knickerbockers with lace-up boots. Some wore straw boaters and waistcoats.

The women's and girls' fashions were more sensible for the heat. They all wore bought-from-catalogue white cotton dresses with hip sashes (with no corsets underneath, or so says my new best mate, who knows these things as he has seven sisters), black stockings and buttoned-over 'Nancy' shoes or lace-up boots.

At first I was a bit shy. George thought it was because I couldn't dance. I told him that I could as Mama had taught us in the kitchen, but that I had only ever danced with her. I didn't mention you, as everyone, including George, thinks you are a boy.

In the end, four young women (as George called them, but they were your age) refused to let me sit idly by tapping my toes. One by one they pulled me onto the dance floor. Two were blonde-braided, freckle-faced sisters from Ballara town up the Corella River, one was the dark-haired daughter of the hotel owner and the other, the prettiest, was the blonde-haired daughter of a Dutchy prospector.

I danced every dance after that and was escorted into a wonderful supper of meat pies, sausage rolls, barramundi, king salmon, grunter and mud crab by all four girls, each one jostling to hold my arms.

Mr McGinness and Mr Fysh have not stopped teasing me about it since. They are calling me a *beau fatale.* I don't know what it means but I told them it was only because I was with the two most popular men in the hall. Which is true—the ladies were queuing up to dance with them. George said it was the uniforms, but George was asked to dance every dance as well.

That's not the half of it, Matt. It has happened! And, as we promised to tell each other, I am telling you now.

I was halfway through dancing the *Pride of Erin* with the prospector's daughter, when she asked me to fetch her a glass of cordial as she was feeling hot. I fetched the cordial and took it to her out in the fresh air.

After she drank it, she turned to me and before I knew what was happening, she kissed me, long and hard. Not on the cheek, Matt. Full on the lips. I could taste the raspberry vinegar and feel the heat from her cheek. Then, while I was trying to catch my breath and stop my heart from thumping so loudly that she would hear it, she kissed me again.

I was wondering how long I would have to hold my breath, when she stopped and asked if I would be her beau and write to her care of the Burketown post office.

Of course I said I would. She is so pretty, Matt, with the bluest of eyes. Although she says my green eyes are very nice too. She even likes the colour of my hair. Her name is Una Bloom, and she is one year older than us. Please do not tell Mama.

Now to what happened after the dance. Just as all the guests were departing for their hotel rooms, homes, tents, humpies, beds in the back of wagons, or bed-rolls on the hotel veranda, a rogue thunderstorm hit the town.

It rolled in from the Gulf, with blueberry-coloured clouds that blotted out the stars, and flashes of silver lightning splitting the sky into a dozen pieces. Mr Fysh thought it would be a dry storm (that's when after all the thunder and lightning, there is no rain) because the wet season up here is from December to March, which is why we are doing this journey now. He was wrong.

The thunder reverberated all the way from the

Selwyn Ranges and back again, sounding like a Salvation Army kettledrum band. The wind became a shrieking gale that rattled and lifted the iron roofs. George had just crawled out from under Lizzie to tie her hood to the cabbage palm so it would not blow off, when all sound and movement stopped.

The silence was eerie. Even the frogs had stopped croaking. Then the sky opened and down pelted the rain.

Soaking wet, George and I raced for the hotel veranda, where we spent the night wrapped in wet blankets, along with a load of drunks from the dance.

Some gambled at two-up all night; others kept on drinking. One was blubbering into his beer that some famous artist called Renoir had died and the world would never be the same; another was toasting Nellie Melba, the greatest singer Australia has ever had; and the third was going on about how it was raining so hard that the fish would be able to swim up the raindrops.

George told them all to shut up as we were trying to sleep. The drunks shouted back. I think there would have been a fight if they could have stood up, which they couldn't.

This morning there wasn't a puddle to be seen. George says the rain will have brought the death adders out of hibernation, and the creeks we are to cross later today will be swollen, so the crocodiles from the gulf will swim further inland.

Have to finish this now as we are departing.

Later—Morning tea at Nicholson River

After taking loads of photographs and waving goodbye to all the friends we'd made, especially my new best mate, who was wearing my best clothes, and Una who had walked the 5 miles into town to see me go, we set off for Turn-off Lagoon police station.

Turn-off Lagoon is 87 miles east of Borroloola and Mr Fysh has calculated that it will take us two days to reach. His plan is to stay ahead of a drover called Higgins who is starting off after us. Higgins has a supply cart and twenty-eight horses which will come in handy if we need to be hauled out of a creek.

George was driving; Mr Fysh was navigating from Mr Smith's map; Mr McGinness was in the back sleeping off a night in the bar of the hotel; and I was sitting on the leather suitcase on the right mudguard watching for rocks that might break our axle, which was already bent from hitting some rocks earlier on, when we had our first puncture of the day.

Here is a secret, Matt. I have been practising kissing the back of my hand and breathing at thc same time, and I think I have got it right. Have you kissed anyone yet?

Later

Another puncture. Every time we get one, I rush around and find firewood, set and light a fire, put the billy on, then continue with your letter.

By 11 am we had crossed the Nicholson River bridge, which is the second we have seen so far and the last we will see for 1,355 miles. Eventually we arrived at Gin Arm Creek which is bigger than Nicholson River. It took us six hours to ford.

We had to unload all the tins of Mobiloil and carry them over a 300 yard sandbank and through the fast running knee-deep water to the very steep opposite side. Next we laid chook netting and branches along the sandbank so Lizzie wouldn't sink. Then George revved up Lizzie, and with Mr Fysh, Mr McGinness and myself pushing, we raced down the sandy bank, along the netted sandbank, through the water, and started up the far side.

But halfway up, Lizzie's tyres slid on the loose sand. George stamped down on the brake pedal and pulled up the handbrake. The bank was so steep that the sudden braking of her back wheels caused Lizzie to almost topple over onto her hood. We all sighed with relief when she slid back into the water, sinking to the tops of her tyres.

Mr McGinness and Mr Fysh dug a ramp which I overlaid with branches and netting. Then George tried a dozen times to drive her through the water and up the other side. Each time she slid back.

I can tell you, George was so red in the face I thought he'd explode, and Mr Fysh used words that would have turned your hair bright red and curl it (if it wasn't curly already). Mr McGinness just laughed. Especially when the car slewed off the ramp and I got a face-full of mud from the whirling back tyres that knocked me backwards into the water.

'Watch out for fresh water crocs,' he warned, then he splashed down beside me and laughed until he cried.

3 September 1919—Brumby River

Three days since I wrote. Today we drove into a herd of brumbies. It was hard to tell which of us was the most surprised, the stallion and his twenty fat mares or the four of us. With a whistling snort the stallion wheeled and the herd was off. George says he reckons they didn't gallop off earlier because they hadn't heard an engine before.

Brumbies are caught by brumby hunters who ship them to India to be sold to the Indian army. Sometimes the blacks, who help catch them, sail with them to keep them calm and to feed them during the journey. Imagine sailing to India!

George said Lord Billy has been to Delhi. I must put Delhi on my list of places to see.

I'm writing this while George mends a leaking tube. Mr Fysh is writing his diary as well. He says my copperplate is very well executed. I told him Mama taught me.

I want to tell you what Mr Fysh told me last night. He was eight years old when the Wright Brothers flew the first aeroplane, and nineteen when he saw his first aircraft, which was the Melbourne to Sydney Mail Service. That's when he knew he wanted to fly more than anything else.

Unfortunately, he wasn't able to learn until the last days of the war, when he gained his Pilot Wings at Heliopolis, Egypt, with only thirty-four hours and fifty minutes solo flying time in his log book. He said he needed a lot more flying hours to catch up with Mr McGinness's five hundred flying hours.

He said he'd chosen Mr McGinness to fly with because Mr McGinness had seven confirmed victories in the air and only one bullet hole in his aircraft. Mr Fysh also wanted a pilot who could land an aircraft on a picket fence if need be, especially if they were on fire, or were being bombarded by Turkish shrapnel or German machine guns. He said that the British Air Command didn't issue parachutes to airmen for fear they would bail out unnecessarily and jettison their expensive aircraft. Imagine going up that high with no parachute?

Mr McGinness butted in then with, 'They needn't have worried, because the moment we saw a Jerry aircraft we turned tail and ran.'

'But only because the BE2E was such an inadequate fighting machine,' interrupted Mr Fysh. (I think he didn't want me to think them cowards, which of course I don't.)

'Inadequate! You mean impossible!' scoffed Mr McGinness. 'Firstly, the BE2E's guns couldn't shoot through their propellers, while the Germans' guns could. Secondly, a BE2E's gunner was in the back seat, so the pilot had to fly alongside the enemy to allow the gunner to aim. And thirdly, if the gunner swung his machine gun round too far he shot through his own tail fin, which made landing difficult I can tell you. Believe me, Jack, BE2Es were a disaster.'

Mr Fysh laughed. Then he explained that a Dutch aircraft designer called Fokker had offered the British his design of a forward-firing machine gun, which fired between the propeller blades by means of an interruptive gear that stopped the propeller for a moment. But the British refused it.

'So Fokker sold it to the Germans,' continued Mr McGinness, 'and the Huns ruled the skies for a year until the British captured a German plane and copied Fokker's design. They then replaced the BE2Es with Bristol Fighters, with double Lewis guns in their rear and Vickers guns firing through their propellers, and that evened things up.'

How fascinating it all sounds. They talk about flying as if it was as easy as walking.

4 September 1919—Turn-off Lagoon

At last we are at Turn-off Lagoon. It took us twice as long as expected.

On arriving, we were greeted by a trooper living in a tin shed beside a billabong full of ducks, magpie geese, pelicans, black swans, spoonbills, cranes, brolgas, jabirus and ibises. We were so dusty and dirty that it was into the lake for a dip. Snake-neck darters darted away, with their bodies under water and their necks and heads sticking up like hundreds of little black periscopes.

While swimming, George and I robbed a duck's nest of four cream-coloured eggs for tomorrow's breakfast. We left two so the ducks won't pine. Then Mr Fysh shot some geese, which the trooper cooked in his camp oven along with the best damper I've ever eaten.

I am writing this as the sun sets over the lake. Pelicans with yellow-rimmed eyes and flapping pink throats are circling overhead, and flocks of white corellas are swooping down to drink the flame-coloured water. A huge butter-yellow moon has bounced into the sky like a child's beach ball. I was about to write to you about how beautiful it all was, when the trooper mentioned that he'd glimpsed Murdering Tommy lurking around the lake two nights back.

Later

I thought I would sleep instantly but the frogs set up a chorus that sounded like Mama's church choir, and every time I closed my eyes I heard something in the bushes; either Murdering Tommy, Kalkadoon warriors or Lord Billy's big animals.

So I have returned to the fire to listen to the men talking about how the Secretary of State for the Colonies in London and the Australian Defence Department didn't know what they were doing when they chose this route for the air race competitors. Mainly because it is uneconomical to get supplies in, as it will take too long, but also because the ground is too uneven and there is no-one to even it up or to build the airstrips.

'And I've got my hands full already,' joked the trooper.

5 September 1919—Westmoreland Cattle Station

Today, like yesterday, we were bogged four times.

The last time, I thought we would be there forever with the tidal water lapping up Lizzie's wheels, when a black boy from the Westmoreland Cattle Station came by. Mr McGinness wrote a note for him to take to the station manager. He must have run like the wind because within an hour, a jackeroo with two horses was pulling us out.

I am beginning to think that the people of Longreach are right—the only way to do this survey is by horse. Not that riding a horse would be any easier than balancing on the back of a rocking, bumping Lizzie.

George isn't keen on horses. Neither is Mr Fysh. When he was a child in Tasmania, he was thrown and dragged along with his foot caught in the stirrup until his body was scratched all over. He said he was still afraid of horses when he worked as a jackeroo on his uncle's sheep farm. When he mentioned that he'd only earned 10 shillings a week, and when he described how cold it was in the mornings, George gave him an odd look.

I don't think George thought Mr Fysh had ever done any hard work.

We are camped beneath an enormous coolabah tree beside the homestead on Westmoreland Station. All around us we can hear the mooing of thousands of penned cattle.

Tomorrow, the owner, along with one black boy and four black women, is setting off with five thousand cattle on his yearly cattle drive to Cloncurry railhead. The owner says the black women are better at mustering than the black men, as they are better at tracking and turning wayward cattle. But he also said that due to the government passing the Aboriginal Wages Award, he was planning on letting go quite a few of his black stockmen. 'Can't afford 'em,' he said. 'Hope they don't hang around here when I do. They'll only cause trouble.'

'Why shouldn't they hang around,' grunted George, when the owner was out of hearing. 'It's their land. And why shouldn't he pay them a decent wage for a decent day's work? It's the right of every man, black or white.'

And woman, I wanted to add. I was thinking about your tiny housemaid's wage.

I will give the owner this letter to post.

Love, Jack.

6 September 1919—Red ant plains

Dear Matt,

Another day of up and down creeks and river banks, only this time Lizzie ran into a termites' nest. The nests are as hard as concrete. Settlers crush them up and make stamped-down earthen floors from them.

The entire plain is covered with them. It looks like a giant's cemetery. The termites are so smart. They build their red dirt tombstone-towers with the wide sides facing east and west to catch the maximum sun, and with the narrow edges facing north and south. So if you are lost you can always find north from a termites' nest.

George, Mr McGinness and Mr Fysh had to prop Lizzie up with rocks, take off her front wheels, straighten her axle by thumping it with the back of an axe, bolt the axle back, and replace the front wheels. I made them a cup of tea, then I did the repacking.

We are heading for Wollogorang Station, which

is on the banks of Settlement Creek about 5 miles into the Northern Territory border, although George said no-one can be sure where the border is. I wonder if we will make it. The bent axle is making steering difficult. Everyone is in a bad mood.

Later

We have arrived at Wollogorang, but only after a punctured tube, followed by being bogged in a creek. Luckily four blacks helped push us out.

The black man is called Big Bob and his wives are Judy, Wanda and Nora, and they all 'belonga Wollogorang'.

They helped push Lizzie out of the water and up the steep bank, from where they watched with astonishment as I cranked Lizzie with the crank-handle. When her engine started with a roar, they galloped back into the creek.

Mr McGinness told them to jump on the running boards and he'd give them a lift into Wollogorang, but they refused to come anywhere near Lizzie now she was 'alive'.

Off we went, but you would not believe our luck. Just as we came in sight of the homestead, we hit a tree stump and bent the axle again.

Off came the wheels, out came the axe, *thump,*

thump, thump. On went the wheels and off we went again, with everyone in an even worse humour, including me, as I had jammed my thumb and it was throbbing painfully. The four blacks were nowhere in sight.

Now we are sitting on the homestead's veranda, which is not in the Northern Territory, but the owner, Mr MacIntosh, says it is so close you could spit into it.

Wollogorang Station is self-sufficient. The old house still has holes in the doors for rifles in case of raids from the blacks. There is an outside laundry, machine house, smokehouse, ringers' and drovers' quarters, house-servants' quarters, and out the back, a cookhouse, where an Oriental gentleman called Jimmy Lou is cooking a feast. I can smell it. I am so hungry I could eat a whole cow, hoofs, skin and all.

Mr MacIntosh boasted that Jimmy Lou is the best cook and gardener in the two states; not like some, he said, who are bad cooks and smoke opium and whom he has punished by chopping off their pigtails and firing them. Chopping off a queue is very upsetting for an Oriental as the Chinese Emperor has decreed that no man from China can cut his hair.

Jimmy Lou and two housegirls tend the station's garden and milk the goats. There are three goats, two nannies and a billygoat called Atilla. Mr MacIntosh says Atilla holds the butting record for both Queensland and the Northern Territory and is the son of another famous billygoat who once ate up an entire church made of grass. Mr MacIntosh says that it takes a brave man to enter Atilla's pen.

Wollogorang Station's vegetable garden is full of tomatoes, sweet potatoes, pumpkins, cauliflowers, pineapples, pawpaws and bananas. Without the garden, Mr MacIntosh says, the station would have to survive on beef.

He says it as if beef is the worst thing in the world to eat, so I didn't mention how seldom we can afford to eat it in Sydney, and how to survive on beef, and not rabbits bought from a rabbito, would be heaven for Mama and Pa.

Now he is telling us scary stories about the olden days so I shall have to write faster.

His first story was about how the blacks set upon the pioneers after the pioneers punished them for spearing their cattle. The pioneers' 'punishment' was to cut off the blacks' ears and nail them around the walls of their slab huts. The blacks' retaliation was to spear the pioneers, burn down their huts, and eat their cattle.

Now he is telling us about the first woman to cross the Barkly Tablelands. Her name was Emily Creaghe. She was twenty-two years old and expecting a baby when she rode the 1,000 miles. It took her six months, riding side-saddle. He didn't say where she had her baby or who she travelled with.

He just stared out into the darkness and said in a ghostly voice, 'Then there's Murdering Tommy creeping around with his spears and his nulla. I wouldn't be surprised if he wasn't camped down with the myalls.'

He told us that the myalls, who are nomadic and not working blacks, such as stockmen or house-maids, were having a corroboree the following night, and he invited us to stay and watch.

I held my breath as I knew Mr McGinness was worried about arriving late in Darwin. Hurrah! Mr McGinness thinks that a day's rest is a good idea.

7 September 1919—Missing housegirls

Today was a lazy day for all of us. We awoke to an air of expectancy about the homestead; an atmosphere of excitement that had the housegirls in a fluster and, half the time, nowhere to be found. Jimmy Lou complained that the two who watered his plants had run away.

Big Bob has come to fetch us, I'll finish this tomorrow.

8 September 1919—Corroboree

I have got up extra early so I can write all this down before I forget one second of it.

An hour before sunset Big Bob came to fetch Mr MacIntosh, Mr Zlotkowski, a refugee from Poland who is Mr MacIntosh's friend, and us. This was because no-one is allowed to enter a myall camp after sundown.

On the way to the camp I asked Mr Zlotkowski what Poland was like. He said not a very nice place just now because the war had devastated it. Especially his city of Warsaw.

As we approached the camp, a tall, thin warrior stepped out from behind a tree. He had long matted hair with a bunch of emu feathers in it, a bone through his nose, possum-skin armlets, and deep-ridged cicatrices across his chest. He was holding a long barbed spear and a corkwood shield, and in his possum-skin belt there were three different shaped boomerangs. Big Bob said he was there to warn us about breaking any laws.

Mr MacIntosh whispered that the ironwood *woora* (shield) and boomerangs had been made especially to match the thrower's height, weight, and length of throwing arm. The ochre snake design painted on his *woora* and boomerangs belonged solely to him, as the snake was his totem, and by painting it, he had put the snake's spirit into his weapons. It also meant he was not allowed to kill or eat snakes.

He whispered that he thought these myalls were an Emu tribe from the Diamantina, which meant they had fire rituals similar to the Possum tribes, whose ancestors first brought fire to the earth. So we would probably see a fire corroboree, although he would rather it was a rain corroboree as his pastures needed a good downpour.

Big Bob told Mr MacIntosh (who he calls bossman) to talk to the bossman rainmaker. By talk, he meant give him sugar, tea, and tobacco. I wonder if the rainmaker can really make rain.

The myalls' camp was set up in a semicircle, with twelve humpies, or gunyahs, facing the lagoon. The gunyahs are built of curved branches and sheets of bark, tied with grass string and twisted kangaroo sinews. Around each was a scooped-out drain in case of a flash storm, and at each entrance there was a prickly bush. Big Bob said that the men slept across the entrance, behind the bush, to protect the women and children in case the tribe was attacked.

Around the semicircle, at quite a distance from the males, sat the young unmarried girls, two of whom were Jimmy Lou's water girls. The girls were shy at the sight of us and they hid their faces behind their hands. Each one had her hair decorated with wanji feathers, plucked from a dancing brolga's wings, and each had fresh incisions cut vertically across her shoulders, chest, belly, and buttocks, rubbed over with layers of clay and charcoal to disinfect them. All the girls held coolamons and *kalori* sticks used for digging up yams.

Big Bob said that they would beat the coolamons with their yams sticks to make music when the sing-song started.

The older women wore hair belts, emu-feathered amulets, grass necklets, and shell charms tied around their necks and arms. Each held two boomerangs. Big Bob said that these were musical boomerangs not 'hit-'em' or 'throw-'em' boomerangs.

In front of the gunyahs, with their backs to the women, sat the men, their bodies and faces covered in ochre and tiny white feathers stuck on with dried blood. Each had a different hairstyle, decorated with feather tufts, dingo and kangaroo bones and head-nets woven from human hair. Most had pierced ears and noses (one had a small screwdriver through his nose) and, being initiated warriors, their front teeth had been knocked out.

With a nod of respect to the elders, which we all copied, Big Bob sat us far enough away from the unmarried girls so as not to offend anyone, while Mr MacIntosh whispered that they had been waiting for us, as it would have been ill-mannered to have started before we arrived. Then the corroboree began.

Softly, like wind coming from a great distance, the older women set up a monotonous high-pitched chant, keeping time by slapping their thighs. The young girls joined in with the *click, click* of their coolamons and yam sticks. Next came an echoing boom from the didgeridoos, followed by the pattering sound of fingers hitting possum-skin and emu-skin drums.

Suddenly, four males leapt out of the darkness. They wore possum-skin aprons, and eaglehawk feathers stuck upright in their clay-covered hair. As they danced, their eagle claws, crocodile teeth, shell necklaces, and seed box armlets and anklets rattled in time to the music.

Each dancer's face, chest, back, and shoulders down to their elbows were banded with tiny duck-down feathers. One wore a tall grass helmet on top of his yellow and white painted face. He looked frightening as he shook his spears at us but then he shook them at all the others and no-one looked afraid.

The dancers stamped their feet in the dust, held their arms out stiff, shook the branches they were holding, leapt high into the air, then stopped with startling abruptness. The dance was over. There was no bowing or applause as with our pantomimes. The performers simply strolled off.

The next dance was a hunting story dance. The men, pretending to be kangaroos, had their hands and faces painted chalk-white, leaving black panda bear circles around their eyes. Their movements were exactly right as they mimed a sitting, listening kangaroo; a scratching kangaroo; a mother kangaroo cuffing her baby's ears.

Then came the hunters, with their bodies covered with kopi paste, and feather and blood patterns picked out in lines. Stealthily, they hunted the kangaroos, who did not see them advancing behind the bushes they held up in front of them. Carefully, they swung their spears across their bodies and pretended to let them fly.

The wounded kangaroos fell to the ground, giving very good imitations of the death throes of a dying animal. The rise and fall of the emu-skin drums, the clop of ceremonial stones, and the rapid beating of the boomerangs reached fever pitch, ending in the victorious swinging of bull-roarers, and again, the sudden stop.

The silence brought me out of my trance. For a few moments I had truly thought I was watching a real kangaroo hunt.

The next dance was a brolga dance. The men's miming of the mincing brolga, jumping in the air and bowing low to attract a mate, was perfect.

So it went on, hour after hour, until Mr MacIntosh told Big Bob that we had to leave. On the way back to the homestead he told us that for blacks, everything that happens, good or bad, is caused by some spiritual being who shares the earth with us, but can only be seen by them.

'So where are these spiritual beings?' I asked.

'In the trees, rocks, grass, sky, earth, rivers, lagoons. Everywhere.'

'Even in our camp,' said George, giving me a nudge.

Everyone laughed except me. Because sometimes when I am in the bush picking up firewood, I am sure I am not alone; that some invisible thing or invisible someone is watching me. But enough of that. I must hurry as I want to tell you more before the others wake up.

After the corroboree, while the men were having their last pipe on the veranda, I decided to go to the vegetable garden and pick myself a pawpaw. Mr MacIntosh had said that I must help myself.

I had just knocked down a large yellow fruit from the nearest tree, when out of the night came a screaming, weapon-wielding apparition dressed in flapping white cloth. I got such a shock (especially after the talk about spirits inhabiting the earth) that I whirled round and raced across the garden with the pawpaw under my arm.

Over the cabbage patch I hurtled, over the beans and peas, over the carrots and cauliflowers, around the chookhouse twice, with the shrieking apparition, which I now realised was a sword-swinging ghost, gaining on me with every leap.

I had thought to jump the fence into the goats' pen and brave the yellow-eyed butting Atilla but the ghost caught hold of my shirt tail.

I was yelling at the top of my lungs and dodging the blows of his sword, when the chicken wire behind me collapsed, and I fell backwards into a yard full of squawking chooks and chook poo. A wet mushy feeling spread over my chest and down my pants.

I truly thought I was wounded, stabbed or sliced in half at least. But when the housegirls rushed out of the kitchen with hurricane lanterns and held them over me, I realised that in my fear I had squashed the pawpaw to a pulp, and that the ghost was a furiously angry Jimmy Lou, who thought me one of the myalls come to steal his fruit.

My yelling had brought the men running. They thought Jimmy Lou had caught Murdering Tommy. How they laughed when they saw me lying in the chookyard with chook poo in my hair and squashed pawpaw all over me.

Jimmy Lou was sent to fetch us each a pawpaw, and I was sent to wash off in the horse trough and then in the washhouse. Which I did. Matt, you should see my bruises, all received from Jimmy Lou's sword, which was his gardening hoe.

This morning I feel so stiff I can hardly walk.

Later

We left Wollogorang early, with Lizzie's back and sides packed high with fruit, vegetables, a huge 25 pound bag of flour for damper, and all our water-bags and bottles full. There are no stations between here and Borroloola and Mr McGinness thinks it might take five or six days to get there.

We crossed Hobble Chain Creek and arrived at Big Running Creek. To cross over this broad creek Lizzie had to drive over two sandhills, down a steep bank, and up an even steeper one.

All looked fine until Lizzie swung out of control on the second sandhill and became bogged. Nothing we did worked, including deflating her tyres and trying to winch her out. Eventually George announced that her radius rods were bent and, you guessed it, her axle. So we decided to camp at Big Running Creek for the night.

Mr Fysh wrote up his diary, I started a fire from the palm fronds lying everywhere, and Mr McGinness set off to capture dinner. He returned with a turkey buzzard which, once plucked, was hung up for the night on a branch of a weeping paperbark.

Apparently gaming birds such as the turkey buzzard are better eaten when they are a little rotten, because it makes them more tasty. (I can see you making a face, I did too.)

In the end George opened some tins of bully beef and we finished with a fruit salad.

9 September 1919—Dingoes at Big Running Creek

When we got up this morning we discovered that the rotting buzzard hadn't been hung high enough, because the dingoes had eaten it while we slept. Makes you wonder what would happen to a bare toe stuck out of a blanket.

Too tired to write more.

10 September 1919—Calvert River

It took us all day yesterday and today to do the 22 miles that brought us to the Calvert River, where we are now. This was because of the thousands of prickly pear trees growing everywhere, and because we were following a drovers' track which was as sandy as Bondi Beach and about as wide.

If we hadn't had the compass and the sun setting in the west I'm sure we would have become lost in the cactus forest. We were digging Lizzie out for the hundredth time, when Mr Fysh said the colour of the sand reminded him of the desert where he'd met Lawrence of Arabia.

I was gobstruck. He had just mentioned the hero I most admire in the world. Only there was no time to ask any questions because he was driving and needed to concentrate. The Calvert River is a deep, fast-moving tidal river which could easily have swept Lizzie away. Fortunately Higgins, with his team of horses, had caught up with us, covering more distance per day than we could cover in Lizzie.

Higgins could have pulled us through, only rather than give in to horse-power, Mr Fysh insisted we wait for the tide to ebb. Then he bumped Lizzie over the rocky river bed in full view of three water-iguanas (freshwater crocodiles) lying on a sandbank, staring red-eyed and gaped-mouthed into our head lamps.

It was on the opposite side that the worst accident of the journey so far took place. Hidden behind the long grass was a ravine three times as deep as Lizzie. As Lizzie raced up the bank and over the sand dune, her left front wheel went into the ravine. Mr Fysh braked immediately and Lizzie hung, shuddering and shaking in the darkness, with a 30-foot drop beneath her, and a white-faced Mr Fysh sitting as stiff as a poker in the driver's seat.

Quickly, Mr McGinness and I jumped onto the right running board while Mr Fysh edged out of the driver's door. Our weight gave George time to lift the winch out of the back, hitch it to a tree, and winch Lizzie onto solid ground.

After this shock we decided to stop where we were for the night. George and I went fishing, and we had a frying pan full of fish when an old blackfella with no clothes, no teeth, but smoking a handsomely carved Indonesian pipe, joined us.

He informed us that he was King Paringi, and that he and his two wives were on walkabout from the big water, because he'd heard we were in the area and he needed some bacca.

The 'big water' was the Gulf of Carpentaria, more than 10 miles north of us.

'A long way to come for a smoke,' said George.

'My bl—y oath,' said King Paringi.

'Call over your wives,' said Mr McGinness.

This was my second shock of the day. His two wives were younger than me and completely naked except for a few leaves, front and back, attached to a possum-skin string. One carried a very smelly dead goanna.

All three smelt of goanna's oil which they had rubbed on their skin to stop the mosquitoes biting. So after Mr Fysh gave them some tobacco and sugar, we were glad to see them and their smelly goanna leave for their walk back to the big water. Not that they went far, we can still see the glow of the old man's pipe further along the creek.

11 September 1919—Warby's Lagoon

This morning we passed Higgins and his horses and we were congratulating ourselves on doing so, when we drove into cypress pine country and lost the track. After that we had to cut down trees and clear away fallen logs so Lizzie could continue west.

Now we are at Warby's Lagoon, where we had the choice of camping beneath a row of blossoming gum trees or in a cypress pine forest. We chose the forest, as the gum trees are full of squealing, blossom-eating flying foxes, hanging like small black umbrellas from the branches and smelling so bad, we couldn't bear it.

George says they excrete while sleeping upside down so it runs down their bodies, but that doesn't deter the blacks, who consider them a delicacy. Aren't you glad you're not a flying fox?

Now comes the worst thing that has happened to me so far.

Before going to bed, I went into the pandanus grass to relieve myself. I was crouching down, when a flock of nankeen herons began shrieking as if they were being attacked by a pack of dingoes. The noise was so close it gave me a shock and I fell backwards; then I felt something bite me. It hurt so much I was sure it was a death adder or a taipan, which meant I would be dead in fifteen minutes.

Without thinking to pull up my under-drawers, I grabbed my trousers and raced back to camp, screaming and yelling that I'd been bitten by a snake. I can see you grinning already.

George flung me over his knee and was about to suck out the snake poison when he shouted, 'You've been bitten on the bum by a bull ant, you silly coot!'

'Will I die?' I yelled.

The three men laughed, I think with relief. For what would they have done with my body? And what would George have told Mama?

The problem is that when a bull ant bites it never lets go, so although I had brushed away its body, its head and jaws were clamped tight to my skin, still causing me pain.

'Have to burn him off,' said George.

I thought he was joking. He wasn't. While Mr Fysh and Mr McGinness held me, George waved a coal so close to my skin it burnt me. It also burnt the ant's head off. He then washed the burn with a solution of Condy's crystals, and now I am lying on my front writing this, with a huge blob of zinc ointment on my bottom, and George chuckling about it every five minutes.

12 September 1919—Somewhere in the middle of nowhere

I have an enormous blister and can't sit or lie down comfortably with Lizzie bouncing around beneath me.

Although it is only 40 miles from Warby's Lagoon to Robinson River, we lost the track many times and had to zigzag back and forth until we found it.

Once again, Higgins and his horses caught up with us. This time he insisted on lending us two horses, Star and Snowy, to drag us out of the worst stretches of sand. He did not mention how much they drink, though, and we were soon short of boiled drinking water and the water we keep to lessen the steam escaping from Lizzie's radiator cap.

Finally, with hardly any water left and with the picture of Bourke and Wills dying of thirst in all our minds, George and Mr McGinness suggested they dig a soak through the bottom of a dry creek bed. They were so deep in the hole they were digging that we couldn't see their heads, when they shouted they'd found water.

As George filled my water bottle he warned me not to gulp the water down too fast (even though I thought I was dying of thirst). Too much water at one time can cause intestinal bleeding which makes a person race around in circles and drop down dead. I sipped my water very slowly after that.

Back in bumping, steaming Lizzie, George explained that sometimes when blacks dig a soak, they find sleeping grey-green and red-capped frogs and even some species of fish that can live indefinitely in the mud, waiting for rain. Australia is a marvellous place, isn't it Matt?

I don't know when this letter will get posted. There are no towns, no drovers and not even a cattleduffer in sight.

George says I should leave it addressed and

stamped on a rock and, with luck, Murdering Tommy will find it and post it for me. He is always making jokes like that.

13 September 1919—Somewhere dry and awful

It is getting harder every day. This morning we had to push Lizzie to get her started. The sand is so clingy that George suggested semi-deflating her tyres. But when we did, the tyres ripped, exposing the tubes which punctured instantly. Next we roped the tyres to the wheel-rims. That failed too.

So while George mended all four tubes and Mr Fysh went hunting, Mr McGinness entertained the invalid (me) with stories of the war, which I will now pass on to you.

Mr McGinness's and Mr Fysh's mission was to fly over Palestine and report on the enemy's movements. They did this three times a week, flying at over 16,500 feet in an open cockpit where the oxygen was so thin they could hardly breathe. They were so cold that Mr Fysh would not have been able to fire his machine gun had they had the misfortune to meet up with the enemy.

He told me all about the pyramids and the Sphinx, and the city of Cairo where all the pilots stayed in a Salvation Army Hostel which had the whitest sheets in the world.

'When you've slept for months in mud, clean sheets are heaven, Jack my boy. And the Salvos had the best food parcels. Oh, how my mouth watered when they handed me one full of chocolate, raisins and, my favourite, condensed milk.'

My mouth watered too just hearing about them. I am sick of salt beef, damper and tough old wallaby.

15 September 1919—Robinson River

I missed a day writing because yesterday my blister was so bad I couldn't sit down, but today it is fine. Now I am covered in mozzie bites.

Lizzie has a cracked windscreen, a wobbly wheel, a bent crankshaft and a clutch that George has to lubricate with engine oil every few miles.

Robinson River is another tidal river, so I am writing while we wait for the tide to drop. From the top of this bank I can see a stony section in the middle which should help us cross. The only problem is, the bank opposite is very steep. I suppose we will have to wade across, hoping there are no crocodiles lurking about, then build a ramp.

Later

We waded across five times, carrying as much as we could to lighten Lizzie's load, then we built the ramp and returned for Lizzie. George had pumped air into her petrol tank to force the petrol to run uphill, as reversing her up the steep far bank was impossible. I cranked her to start her engine, then with Lizzie revved and shaking to go, Mr McGinness and I jumped on her back and we were off, with Mr Fysh riding Star and leading Snowy beside us.

We were speeding towards the stony bank when I saw the crocodile. It was at least 16 feet long, which is twice as long as my bedroom in Sydney. It was lying with its nostrils and eyes barely sticking out of the water, exactly where George and I had waded only five minutes earlier.

'Crocodile!' I shouted, as Lizzie hit the water.

The next thing I heard was a gunshot. The horses bolted as, with water spraying out on both sides, Lizzie hit the rocky bank. Then, as if she knew there was a croc snapping at her tyres, she churned through the water and up the ramp, with George swearing like a trooper, Mr McGinness hanging onto the hood, and me jumping up and down beside him yelling at the top of my voice, my blister completely forgotten.

Mr McGinness said he'd seen the crocodile at the same time as I had, but he didn't think he'd hit it as he hadn't had time to aim properly.

George thinks the crocodile got us because there is a dent in the driver's door which looks like a very large crocodile's tail has slapped it, and I remember a tremendous bang as we hit the rocky bank.

It took half an hour for Mr Fysh to coax the horses across, and only because Mr McGinness was sitting on the bank with his rifle ready. Not that the horses understood this.

Our food supply is dangerously low. There are no kangaroos or wallabies to shoot, so to celebrate not being eaten by the crocodile, Mr Fysh prepared a stew of parrots (the toughest bird in the bush), a crane, a bush pheasant and three leatherheads (and leather-tasting they were too).

He said he had prepared a similar pie for his school mates when he was at boarding school in Geelong.

Here is the recipe:

Cook birds with two stones. Boil until stones are soft, then boil one more hour to make birds ready to eat. Throw away the birds and drink the stone soup.

16 September 1919—Fulch River

Today was so dreary, with so many dry creek beds to negotiate and so many punctures to mend, that if Mr Fysh hadn't begun talking about Gallipoli again I think I would have fallen asleep with boredom.

This time he talked about his mate, John Simpson Kirkpatrick, who risked his life every day going onto the battlefield with Duffy, his donkey, to fetch the wounded. Then, when Simpson (as they called him) was shot, how a brave soldier raced out to fetch him.

He described the trenches that the Australian infantry lived in for weeks on end; how they were protected from machine-gun snipers by rows of sandbags; how the soldiers deloused their clothing by running a lighted match up and down the seams; and how they would make a run through the enemy's bullets to get to the Aegean Sea for a swim, just to feel clean, even if the water was freezing.

He talked about his feet aching from the frostbite and about a bomb exploding at his feet and a lump of red-hot metal going through his water bottle instead of him.

'Killed the bottle I'm afraid,' he said, without a smile. It's odd the way Mr Fysh talks about the war, all serious and quiet; whereas Mr McGinness tells funny stories. Such as when everyone was told to sew white patches on the backs of their uniforms to distinguish them from the enemy. But as no-one had any white material, they chopped up their under-drawers for the patches.

Fulch River was running high. We crossed it with the help of the horses. Mr Fysh and Mr McGinness were too tired to go hunting, so George has made a damper and we are scraping out the golden syrup tin. Mr McGinness says that tomorrow he'll shoot a kangaroo. But we haven't seen any for a few days.

17 September 1919—Snake Lagoon

I am writing this in the twilight beside Snake Lagoon. It is a beautiful place, full of waterlilies and surrounded by peeling paperbarks. Above me are two frogmouth owls making their *moo* calls, and I thought that if I had a choice of a tribal totem, the bird or animal that I was before I became a human, I would choose the frogmouth owl. I wonder if twins have to have the same totem? I imagine you more as a brush-tailed possum.

There are more bird species here than I have seen anywhere else. There are squawking magpie geese, purple-black lotus birds with widespread feet balancing on the lily pads, flocks of galahs and spoonbills, and so many yellow-tailed and flame-spotted cockatoos that when they whirl they blot out the sun.

George says the blacks consider the cockatoos sacred because cockatoos never fly more than 5 miles from water. They call them the thirsty man's bird and use their feathers for their water-totem ceremonies. I don't think I will ever look at a cockatoo without remembering that.

Mr Fysh shot a wallaby and some ducks and then he and Mr McGinness went for a swim. But even though George and I know the lagoon is not connected to the sea, we didn't go in. As George says, 'All that's needed is one long-distance walking croc and we'd be goners.'

I am becoming fond of Star and Snowy. I suppose it is because I am responsible for them. I hobble them at night and catch them in the mornings. Mind you, I could never love them the way I love Lizzie. Poor, battered Lizzie. She is looking the worse for wear, with her black duco so scratched it looks grey.

George is calling me. He says with a name like Snake Lagoon we are probably surrounded by pythons, taipans and king browns. He says that king browns can kill a dog.

George has shown me how to kill a snake. I must grab it by the tail, flick it up, and bash its head on a rock. So far I haven't seen any, and I am glad, as I don't know if I could grab one by its tail.

18 September 1919—Werrin River

What a day! We had crossed the Werrin River with no problems when things began to go wrong. Lizzie's clutch band started to loosen every few hours due to so much shaking about and George having to drive so far in low gear.

Next, the fan kept hitting the radiator so the radiator needed patching, which George is doing now. He is melting sulphur in a saucepan on the fire and intends tipping it into the hole to make it leakproof.

But the worst thing is that we only have 4 gallons of Mobiloil left and we are still 30 miles from Borroloola.

George is going on about how Model T Fords need more speed gears; that slow, fast and reverse isn't enough; and that they need keys, like a front door key, to switch on their engines, because having to crank up an engine to start is too slow. Now there's a thought. Hard to imagine starting Lizzie with a front door key.

19 September 1919—The never-never

Where the crows fly backwards to see where they've been.

Today we drove 21 miles. Of course there were plenty of creeks. Plenty of unpacking. Plenty of repacking. And more mosquitoes. But what I hate the most are the tiny bush flies.

They get into my eyes, up my nose, in my ears, down my shirt, up my trouser legs, and, if George isn't fast enough while cooking, they cover the meat in a black glistening mass or drown themselves in our billy tea.

20 September 1919—Back of the never-never

I have axe handle blisters. Today was spent cutting down acacia and bloodwood trees to make a track. It was a shame to cut the trees. The bloodwoods are covered with silver flowers like tiny stars, and the acacias' fluffy yellow blooms were full of native bees.

I told everyone that where we live in Leichhardt there aren't any trees, and that Mama says if we keep cutting them down there will be no fresh oxygen, because trees make oxygen. George grunted at this, but Mr McGinness said Mama is right.

Later

Fletcher River at last. Mr McGinness reckons that since we left Burketown we have crossed six tidal rivers and over forty creeks. He worked out that the horses have pulled us 20 miles, so they are worth their hay, not that they get any.

21 September 1919—Well past Fletcher River

We left the Fletcher River at dawn. Our speed was slow as Lizzie's radius rods are bent so badly it is hard to steer her straight.

Mr Fysh was trying to avoid a tree when Lizzie went into a skid and hit it, resulting in a bent front axle, an even more damaged radiator and a snapped fan spindle.

For a few minutes we just sat there feeling completely frustrated, then George heaved out his bag of tools, opened up Lizzie's bonnet, and announced he'd be a few hours.

After I made tea for everyone, Mr McGinness and Mr Fysh decided to teach me the finer points of cricket. Mr Fysh played rugby and VFL football for Geelong Grammar, but his favourite game is cricket.

Mr Fysh bowled a ball made out of old newspaper and twine and Mr McGinness hit it with the frying pan. I fielded. Then I got to bowl and bat. It was as hot as an oven and George said we were acting like village idiots. But it lightened our mood and made us laugh.

I was fielding a six when I saw bees buzzing in and out of a knothole up in a dead tree. Mr McGinness said he would hoist me up to get the honey, but I refused until I was dressed in Mr Fysh's pith helmet with fly-netting tied over it and around my neck and with a tarpaulin over my shoulders for protection. Then Mr McGinness and Mr Fysh lifted me onto their shoulders and I attacked the knothole with a tomahawk.

One chop and the bees came swarming out of the tree and all over me. I kept chopping and soon had a hole large enough to put my hand in and scoop out the honey and honeycomb, which I was to put in a bucket tied to my trouser belt under the tarpaulin. This was not easy and the bees got in with the honey, but I wasn't stung because native bees do not sting like European bees do.

The honey tasted wonderful, and the three of us were congratulating ourselves when George shouted that Lizzie was ready to go. So I will finish this later. Sorry about the sticky honey stains.

Later—Feathertop Creek

We continued on without the cooling fan, which meant stopping every time the engine overheated. But even so, we broke our daily record and travelled 22 miles to Feathertop Creek. Eight miles more and we would have reached McArthur River and Borroloola, but we were too tired to push on.

22 September 1919—McArthur River

On reaching McArthur River we found the sand was so deep that Lizzie could not plough through it, no matter how Mr McGinness revved her.

Attracted by our noise, some blacks appeared, paddling canoes hollowed out of Leichhardt pines (I didn't know there was a pine tree named after Leichhardt). George asked them what they were catching and they shouted back, 'Gropers, sharks and crocodiles.'

One cheeky boy shouted that the gropers were so large they could pull a canoe along. So George shouted back, 'Can you get one to help heave us out of this sand?'

They laughed so much I thought their canoes would capsize. Then five muscular men came ashore and, with no effort, pushed Lizzie to a ford where they helped build a ramp to get her up the other side.

This pushing and digging was watched by the rest of the tribe, who considered it great entertainment. Their language is very musical. It sounds like water running over rocks. George says there are so many different tribal languages all over Australia that if the blacks didn't have a universal sign language they wouldn't be able to communicate with each other. He says their sign language could fill a dictionary.

After all that pushing, we decided to make camp even though Borroloola was probably within cooee distance, or so guessed George.

23 September 1919—Borroloola, place of paperbark

Well, we did it! We drove the first automobile from Burketown to Borroloola. True it took much longer than Mr McGinness thought it would, but we have crossed (with the help of the horses) 355 miles of parched desert country driving an average of 16 miles a day, our worst day being 6 miles.

What a relief it was to stagger (if an automobile can stagger, and Lizzie can) into the tiny four-house township of Borroloola, with our horses limping behind us and only 3 gallons of Mobiloil left.

When we pulled up outside the pub, everyone came out on the veranda to stare. The hotel owner, a Mr Lynott (who looked about a hundred years old) shook hands with us and greeted us with, 'I am glad to see ya, cobber. What do you know about the strikes?'

'What strikes?' asked George.

'The Broken Hill Miners' and the Seamen's Union strikes.'

'Not a bl—y thing. We've been in the desert for twenty-two days.'

Borroloola has very few white inhabitants. It began as a watering stop during the 1886 Halls Creek gold rush. Later on, when crocodile skin boots and handbags became fashionable, it became a trading centre for the young men who came down from Darwin to try a bit of crocodile hunting. Now it is a supply depot for the Gulf's settlers.

The police officer is confident that all this will change now that the Versailles Peace Conference has taken New Guinea away from the Germans (because they lost the war) and given it to Australia (because we won). He reckons that as Borroloola is the closest town to New Guinea, it's going to put Borroloola on the map.

'What map?' joked George.

I wonder what the New Guinea people think of this giving away of their country.

24 September 1919—Still Borroloola

This morning Mr McGinness said that by his calculations the worst of our journey was over. I hope he is right. I am fed up with sand.

Since we arrived yesterday, Lizzie has undergone an enormous amount of work. Her radiator had to be repaired and a new fan spindle and blade made. Her fan arm, front axle, steering arm, starting handle and radius rods had to be straightened, and the radius rods encased in iron sheeting to prevent more bending. Her speedometer driving wheel is a problem, but a Reverend Warren, from Roper River Mission Station, says he can make a new part from a horseshoe, as he'd done it for his own automobile.

George wants to replace a back wheel, bolt her mudguards on anew as they have almost been shaken off, strengthen the running boards with a plank bolted under her chassis, tighten up all her nuts and bolts, and buy a new axe handle to replace the splintered one. The axe has proved to be our most important mechanical tool.

What has survived the trip is: the canvas top, the front lights, carriage lights, windscreen which is cracked but still in place, and horn, which was only used to amuse the blacks or to frighten away the blue-cheeked emus.

Emus are the most curious of birds; they are always wandering in front of Lizzie, staring at her eye to eye (or eye to headlamps) as if challenging Lizzie's right of way.

The blacks call emus drought predictors because an emu will not lay eggs if a drought is coming. So, no eggs means no rain. Also, it is the male emu that sits on the eggs and brings up the striped chicks, which tiptoe after him until they grow up. Odd, isn't it? I wonder what all the mothers in Sydney would do with their time if they didn't have babies to bring up?

Enough about emus. I am listening to Mr Fysh and Mr McGinness composing a telegraph to the Defence Department saying that Borroloola is quite isolated, with no sea or road communications, and turpentine and cypress trees that are too tall to cut down and remove; that the ground is covered with saucer-shaped gilgai holes which would have to be filled in; and that there are no willing locals looking for work.

George says that blacks say gilgai holes are what's left after the moon's tears hit the ground.

25 September 1919—Still in Borroloola

George is still mending Lizzie. The people say that the mail boat is due any day now so I shall be able to send you a letter, although it won't reach you for a month or six weeks. Please remember, just because I am having the adventure of my life it doesn't mean I don't miss you, because I do.

The people here are not at all interested in Mr Fysh's and Mr McGinness's aerial service, which wouldn't land here anyway because it is too far north. They say they'd rather have a railway line. George says it will be over a hundred years before there are enough people up here to make a railway line profitable.

26 September 1919—Borroloola mail boat

I am getting to know Borroloola from back to front. It is smaller than Burketown, so the mail and supply boat only comes every four or six months, depending on the weather and the tide. But when it arrives, as it did this morning, what a celebration there is. At the sound of its foghorn the whole town came running.

The whole town includes the inhabitants of its four houses, the owner of the hotel, the storekeeper, the police officer, the drovers and settlers who have ridden in to pick up goods, and the blacks, who live on the opposite side of the river.

The blacks are of the Yanyula, Garrawa, Mara and Kurdandji people, who have settled there. By their confident manner, I get the feeling they are in charge; that the settlers are living on the edge of their town, not the other way round.

Mr McGinness said that we timed our arrival perfectly, as we would have had to wait for the supply boat's arrival to pick up our Mobiloil.

The captain pulled in close to the shore as there is no jetty, then all the mail and goods were thrown onto the bank at the feet of the waiting people.

This morning, there was a black-lead kitchen range and a fancy wooden dresser (not thrown but lowered), dozens of crates, two holding our cans of Mobiloil, three butter churns, a bundle of scrubbing boards roped together, and a mountain of parcels. Nothing was stolen. I suppose it is because the place is so small, the culprit would soon be caught.

I will give the captain of the supply boat this

very large letter to post to you as I do not know when I shall have the chance again. Give Mama and Pa a big hug from me, and tell them the news.

Love, Jack.

27 September 1919—Billy of Borroloola

Dear Matt,

The supply boat has gone and I have some special news. The hotel owner has given me a puppy which I have called Billy, after Lord Billy, because he is black.

Billy is the runt of the litter. George says he won't live, but I shall make sure he does. George also says he doesn't know what Mrs Banks will say as she is not 'animal-minded'.

Yesterday, after the boat left, the settlers and us played cricket against the blacks and I bowled out three. The blacks won. They are great cricketers. George played then he went back to fixing Lizzie.

Two of the boys have invited me to their camp for some tucka tonight.

Later

It is very late and I am writing this by the light coming from the pub window; I don't want to forget anything and we are leaving early tomorrow morning.

Billy and I were taken across the river by canoe with the two boys paddling. I kept my hands inside in case of crocs.

Once at the camp, my freckles were examined and my red hair, which has grown quite long, was patted and plucked out to be added to hair string which will be finger-knotted into a dilly bag.

There were plenty of healthy looking dingo-like dogs in the camp, so I showed their owners my sick Billy. They said he needed 'feeding up'.

The boys' mother taught me how to feed him by sticking my little finger first in beef fat and then halfway down his throat so he can't spit it out, and how to chew meat until it's soft, then put it bit by bit into his mouth. Up until now I have been feeding him condensed milk from a spoon. Most of it ends up on me.

The boys showed me how to set snares for kangaroos and wallabies for when they come down to drink at the river, and how they catch freshwater prawns with lumps of meat. I told them that's how we caught yabbies. Then they tried to teach me how to pick up a stone with my toes while running, flick it up and catch it in my hand, and hurl it accurately enough to hit a possum.

I couldn't even pick the stone up with my toes

while standing still. This caused them great merriment, so I had to wrestle the biggest one to prove I could do something they couldn't do. Blacks don't wrestle. But they do box. I was lucky not to have come home with a blood nose.

For tea I had blackfella tukka. Large brown mantises skewered together on a stick and edible roots baked with *ka-ko-ma,* which is a small mole that has no ears or eyes but has a thick leathery snout for digging and a lovely golden pelt used for making rugs.

I wasn't keen on the mantises after I was told how these stick-like creatures climb into bird's nests and suck the blood out of the little birds' breasts. And I didn't like eating the *ka-ko-ma* even though it was delicious. I felt sorry for the little creatures. Fancy being blind, deaf, and eaten.

The boys' father and uncle brought me back across the river. The boys were afraid to leave the camp at night. They are afraid of *Yamma-coona,* a spirit-woman who lives in the Milky Way, which they call the Belt of *Balleroo,* the rain god.

Yamma-coona has all the souls of all living things tied to her left hand by an invisible, unbreakable silken thread. With this thread she spins the lives of her humans. When a thread snaps she flings out her net and gathers in the human's soul. She captures settlers' souls too. She spins her spells and keeps them enslaved to the land they've fenced in.

Even the men were nervous as they paddled me home. *Yamma-coona* has been known to take an entire canoe in her net.

I didn't get back until midnight. I found the men sitting on the hotel veranda, talking about the war again. It's as if they can't leave it alone. They worry at it like a dog with a bone, or like the green moths worry the hurricane lamps hanging over their heads.

All of them, except Mr Fysh, and Mr McGinness and George, were foot soldiers in Ypres, France, where they'd spent months climbing through barbed wire, shooting at the Germans, or sleeping in muddy trenches surviving on not enough bully beef, army biscuits and runny jam, and going to the privy wherever they couldn't be shot at. All of them remembered mates that didn't come back.

I heard one returned soldier say that out of 33,000 Australian volunteers only three in every ten came home. So it's no wonder they were sad.

While listening to the men and writing this letter, I found out how Mr Fysh and Mr McGinness met Lawrence of Arabia.

The first time, they almost killed him. It was when they were attempting to bomb a battalion of Turkish cavalry who were occupying a crusader's castle in Kerak. That's right, a crusader's castle with turrets and drawbridge like you see in picture books.

The second time was in the desert, when Mr Fysh had to deliver a message from the British High Command. After they landed, Mr Fysh said he'd thought they would never be allowed to take off again, as they were surrounded by gun-firing, yelling Arabs, galloping around on camels. But Lawrence of Arabia had lifted his hand, the noise stopped, and they took off in complete silence.

Mr McGinness told a funny story about how they'd made a forced landing near Jericho after bombing some Turkish dhows (boats) that were taking grain to the Germans, and how Mr Fysh had talked an Arab storekeeper into selling them some fuel to enable them to take off again.

'Had to give him my watch,' said Mr Fysh. 'The one that hadn't worked since I'd gone swimming with it on.'

I was dying to ask if they meant the Jericho that's in the Bible; the one where the walls fall down at the sound of the war trumpets. But I was supposed to be asleep so I have put Jericho down on my list of places to go after Shanghai, Delhi, Cairo, the Dead Sea and Poland.

Oh no! Billy has widdled inside my shirt. He's not quite trained yet.

It must be 1 am at least, my hand is almost falling off with writing so much so I'm off to bed now. The men are still talking and smoking.

28 September 1919—Still Borroloola

We were to leave Borroloola today but we are leaving tomorrow. I think it is because everyone, including me, went to bed so late. I'm sure I would have slept till midday only Billy widdled on me again and woke me up.

29 September 1919—Somewhere on the Gulf

Our first day travelling west towards Roper River was uneventful until this afternoon, when we came across the Reverend Warren, the same man who helped us make a new speedometer wheel from a horseshoe.

He was stuck in a creek so we pulled him out. His Model T Ford is in far worse condition than Lizzie, which isn't surprising, as he has driven it from Melbourne, through four states, all the way to the Gulf.

Mr Fysh and Mr McGinness invited the

Reverend to eat with us. George was a bit put out because the flour we'd bought in Borroloola has weevils in it. It became my job to pick them out. He said if he'd realised earlier he could have put the flour out in the sun and the weevils would have left it voluntarily. Reverend Warren said he had eaten weevils before and they were nutritious.

Weevils apart, George produced a fine salt-beef stew and damper followed by dumplings and golden syrup which we all enjoyed, including Billy.

30 September 1919—Dry plains and scanty bush

You will never believe what happened last night.

As we have no tents, Mr McGinness and Mr Fysh slept under a tarpaulin stretched out from Lizzie. George, Billy and I slept under Lizzie's wooden floor boards between her wheels, to avoid waking up wet from dew.

During the night, I woke up. I thought Billy, who sleeps tucked under my arm, had woken me. Then I felt something slithering up my chest. I held my breath and prayed that Billy wouldn't move as the thing slithered out of my blanket, up past my neck and past my ear. It was a snake as long as myself and as round as my wrist. I saw its glittering eyes and heard its hiss as it wriggled over to where George was snoring his head off. I was so scared I almost squashed Billy.

Once it was off me I called to George, 'George, George don't move. There is a snake in bed with you.'

I called four times before he whispered back, 'Where?'

'Heading for your legs.'

For what felt like a long time, we both lay still and silent. Then George sat bolt upright, bashing his head on the bottom of Lizzie. With a shout of pain he wriggled out from under her. I crawled out behind him.

Our noise woke Mr Fysh and Mr McGinness who, hearing the word 'snake', quickly lit the hurricane lamps and began circling Lizzie.

'What are you looking for?' I asked.

'Its mate,' said George, rubbing the huge egg on his forehead. 'There is always a mate.'

So there we were, in the middle of the night in the middle of the bush, searching for a snake. We didn't find it. The amazing thing was that Reverend Warren, who was asleep in his Model T Ford next to Lizzie, slept through everything.

We have decided to drive in tandem as it is unlikely Reverend Warren will get through without our help.

The Reverend knows about aeroplanes. He told me how biplanes are built of wood, with wire-braced wings made of fabric as light as thistledown. He said flying was best done early morning or late afternoon, as the heat of the sun warped the aircraft's wooden frames and the turbulence of the hot air made the pilots airsick.

Mr McGinness and Mr Fysh never mentioned airsickness.

'Of course, that has changed, and will change more,' the Reverend continued. 'Look at our Model T Fords. Twelve years ago they didn't exist. Now we are driving across a continent, and the Prince of Wales is flying from Spain to Germany to attend a dance given by the occupying Canadian and American armies.'

2 October 1919—Limmen River

I didn't write yesterday because there was no time, and nothing of interest happened other than being bogged.

We are camped at a distance from the Limmen River because it is full of crocodiles. Reverend Warren said that he knew a hunter who'd shot fifty-seven crocs from near here.

This information made George very leery. He

thinks we should sleep in Lizzie. He says crocodiles have longer memories than elephants.

This is uninhabited country—no-one for hundreds and hundreds of miles—only gritty, sandy plains covered in stunted gidgee trees and salt bush and in the distance, a row of flat-topped mountains, their edges outlined in flaming orange from the setting sun.

Reverend Warren says that I'd be amazed what one good soaking will do; that there will be a carpet of purple wild-carrot plants, lilac-coloured desert roses, scarlet desert pea, spider lilies, wild marigolds and paper daisies for as far as the eye can see. I can't imagine it.

But I have seen mirages. They tricked me at first, but now I know it isn't possible to find cities, palm trees, or green forests out here in the desert, even though I saw them glimmering on the horizon.

The track we're travelling on is called the Gulf Road. It got its name in 1886 when it was travelled by the thousands of prospectors rushing to find gold at Hall's Creek.

Before that, when Ludwig Leichhardt travelled the 3,000 miles from Brisbane to Port Essington in 1845, this desolate wasteland had no track and no name. Although I imagine the blacks had a name for it.

George says to look out for a tree marked with 'L' beside the Nathan River. But which of the many dry creeks that we have driven in and out of is the Nathan River?

3 October 1919—Limmen Bight

When we awoke this morning, Mr Fysh and Mr McGinness suggested that while George helps Reverend Warren straighten out his radius rods again, they should drive north to Limmen Bight to trade for some fresh fish with the coastal blacks.

Mr McGinness and Mr Fysh took their guns in case they saw a water buffalo or a crocodile. Billy and I went too. George said they could use Billy for bait. Billy has been at George's boots again. He thinks they are a dead kangaroo. Mr McGinness says it's because they smell like a dead kangaroo. George was not amused.

Later

We didn't reach the gulf. Limmen River turned into an evil-smelling, black-oozing mangrove swamp. I saw tiny tree-climbing fish flopping across the mud to reach the mangrove roots, where they clung goggle-eyed and shivering. Mr Fysh said the mud crabs would eat them. Everything eats everything up here.

We were no sooner back when Billy decided to go walkabout while I was building the fire. I spent a frantic half hour searching for him. He likes to crawl down rabbit holes, so I was digging one out when I found a bilby nest.

Bilbies are desert bandicoots the size of rabbits. They eat plants, insects, and spiders. Although what they find to eat out here I cannot guess; probably tree-climbing fish and curious black puppies.

There were three babies curled up head to tail in the nest. They had long pink ears, long pink tails and soft grey fur. George warned me not to touch them or the mother might not come back, so I didn't.

Billy was in a hollow log eating white ants. He will eat anything. I wish you could see him. He has a wet black nose, a wet pink tongue, two big brown eyes and two floppy black ears. When he is older I am going to train him to be a rabbiter. George says he's so small he'll probably end up a cockroacher.

4 October 1919—Hodgson Downs

We left Limmen River and its crocodiles at sun-up. After an exhausting day of crossing the Cox River and straightening Reverend Warren's radius rods every mile, we arrived at Hodgson Downs at sundown. Reverend Warren's radius rods are about finished. Meanwhile Lizzie's engine, thanks to George's work in Borroloola, is going beautifully.

Hodgson Downs homestead is a lonely place in the middle of the Roper Valley. It has a wire rabbit-proof fence to protect a scraggly garden, a surly-faced manager, and a fencer whose family lives in a lopsided tin shanty down by the creek.

The fencer has a wife, who George says looks twenty years his senior (life out here is very hard for women), and three daughters: barefoot, sun-bleached, white-haired and bilby-shy, with eyes of such a pale blue they look almost white in their sunburnt faces.

Amy, Dolly and Polly are aged twelve, ten and eight. Amy chews her hair the way you do, and Dolly and Polly suck their thumbs. All three wear dresses made of sugarbags.

Eventually Amy bucked up courage to talk to me and I showed her Billy. That broke the ice, so while the men talked, the girls showed me their collection of farthings which they keep in a

Bushels Tea tin buried beside four wooden crosses. These are the graves of their brothers and sisters, all dead before they turned one year old.

I said it was sad that they'd died, but Amy shrugged and said matter-of-factly, 'Poppa can't feed seven children anyway.'

Later that evening Reverend Warren said a prayer over each grave. It made the girls' mother cry.

I think I am becoming tired of travelling.

5 October 1919—Hodgson Downs

Today, while George switched the tyres around and tinkered with Lizzie's engine (there's a knock he can't find the source of), and Mr Fysh and Mr McGinness went hunting, Amy, Dolly, Polly and I played hide-and-seek amongst the turpentine bushes and the graves. The one caught had to suffer prickly grass stuffed down the back of their neck.

We also played a game of quoits with old horseshoes. As you know, I am good at this game, but not as good as Dolly. She never missed once. George says it's because there is not much else for the poor little mites to do up here.

While I was with the girls, Billy chewed

George's bootlaces to a pulp. George says if he catches him, he'll make a stew of him.

6 October 1919—West of Cox River

We left Hodgson Downs this morning. Amy gave me a potato bag to keep Billy in. I gave her some writing paper as they don't have any. She has asked me to write to her. That's two penpals I have, other than you and Mama.

During our stay at Hodgson Downs, Reverend Warren, who knows as much about automobiles as George, made some new radius rods from his old ones and our old ones. It was a three-hour job, but it worked.

We are going as fast as we can, as Mr Fysh and Mr McGinness want to catch the weekly train from Katherine to Darwin.

8 October 1919—Roper River

It has taken us two days to reach Roper River, which is quite low. Reverend Warren says during the wet it becomes impassable and the plains turn to mire. He has seen a horse bogged to its shoulders and a bullock drowned in the mud.

George and I made camp amongst the trees beside a sandbar which we will cross tomorrow.

Mr Fysh and Mr McGinness rode off on the horses beside Reverend Warren's sick automobile. They are going to escort him to his mission which is off our route.

The country around here is a popular meeting place for blacks. Surrounded by canegrass twice the height of a man, the tribes exchange kangaroo-skin cloaks, cured kangaroo-skin waterbags, Cloncurry blue diorite axes, flint-flake chisels, spearheads, blue flax dillybags, spinifex grass glue, red and yellow ochre for corroborees, magpie geese feathers, seed necklaces, puppies, and acceptable partners for marriage.

It must look like Paddy's Market in Haymarket.

The canegrass is a good place for the blacks to hide, as a policeman's horse cannot negotiate the hidden bogs, mud pools, or the saltwater channels where hungry crocodiles lurk.

'I bet Murdering Tommy is out there,' said George. 'Reverend Warren said this is Tommy's tribal land.'

'When they catch him what will happen to him?' I asked.

'They'll lock him up in Fannie Bay Gaol, where he'll die of a broken heart like a caged animal.'

I asked if he didn't think what Murdering

Tommy had done was wrong.

'Of course it was wrong. But who is to know what terrible wrong was done to Murdering Tommy in the first place?'

Then he puffed on his pipe and added, 'Anyway I don't reckon the police will get him. I reckon it'll be the Elders of his tribe. All his tribe are blood-oath kinsmen. Any wrong done to a tribal brother or sister or wrong done by a tribal brother or sister, is done by or to the whole tribe. So the tribe is honour-bound to avenge these injuries or, in this case, to punish Murdering Tommy if they think he was wrong.'

'How will they punish him?'

'Point the bone I reckon. Then he'll lay down and die. There's no way of avoiding a pointed bone.'

George told me this while he made the damper. Beyond the fire everything was as dark as ink; I could hear the *swish, swish* of the cane grass's fluffy tops. From the other side of the river came the splashing and wallowing noises of a herd of buffalo. Close by I thought I heard a soft footfall.

One thing is for sure, if it is Murdering Tommy, neither George nor I are armed other than with the carving knife George uses to slice up the kangaroos and wallabies for cooking.

But then I don't suppose George would use it.

He would probably hunker down and have a good chat with Murdering Tommy before giving him a cup of tea, a sandwich, and a bottle of Aspro to avoid the pointed bone.

Mr McGinness and Mr Fysh returned by boat. They have left Star and Snowy at the mission, as we won't need them. I would have liked to have said goodbye to them. Everyone is wishing the tide would go down faster so we can get going. Katherine is very close.

I asked them if they had heard anything about Murdering Tommy at the Mission. They said they hadn't but if the crocs didn't get him, the police would.

It must be very sad to be hunted in your own tribal land.

9 October 1919—Leichhardt's Bar

We left Roper River this morning, and without the help of the horses and without too many stops, we reached a place called Leichhardt's Bar. George says he doesn't reckon Leichhardt made it this far, but Mr Fysh said rumour had it that someone saw Leichhardt this far north and that he was living with a tribe of blacks.

11 October 1919—Katherine at last

We are in Katherine at last and I am 5 pounds richer, as Mr Fysh handed it over the second we arrived. It took three days to reach here from our camp on the Roper River and fifty-four days to cover the 1,354 miles from Longreach to Katherine, not the twenty-eight days Mr McGinness surmised.

Lizzie is to go by goods train to Darwin where George says he is going to pull her apart and rebuild her. We four are departing on 'Leaping Lena', the passenger train, in a few minutes, so let me quickly describe Katherine.

The land is flat and the town is scattered over a large area, with a broad, dusty main street going right down the centre. The population is mostly blacks, with a scattering of whites and a few Afghan cameleers. It is quite normal for one Afghan cameleer to take ten or more fully-laden camels all the way from Katherine to Alice Springs.

The stationmaster boasted that 40 miles north there is a most wonderful gorge full of scarlet rocks and sparkling blue water. Mr McGinness joked that we could all do with some sparkling blue water as we are very hot and dusty.

13 October 1919—Darwin

We have arrived in Darwin (population 1,200). I slept for almost the whole train ride, waking only when the train stopped at Pine Creek and Palmerston. George said I was probably exhausted. It is very exciting to be in the topmost town of Australia.

There was a large crowd waiting to cheer us when we retrieved Lizzie. The newspapers had been telegraphed that we were coming and they had alerted their readers.

The reporters followed us to the Victoria Hotel where Mr Fysh and Mr McGinness were interviewed. Everyone said our journey was a miracle. Mr Fysh and Mr McGinness said that George was the miracle. I think so too.

The whole of Darwin is buzzing about the air race. The reporters kept asking us who we thought would win. Mr Fysh said they were all good men.

Posting this and my other letters today.

Love, Jack.

14 October 1919—Still Darwin

Dear Matt,

I have picked up your and Mama's letters from

the post office (which has been here since 1871) and posted mine to you. It is from this post office that the under-sea telegraph cable connects Australia with Java and then the rest of the world. That is how the news of the air race will be received before being sent on down the Overland Telegraph Line to the rest of Australia.

I am very pleased you got a part in the Christmas play, and that Mrs Wentworth is allowing you time off to rehearse. I know you will make a marvellous angel and that Mama will make you a beautiful costume. Good luck.

Darwin is built high up on a promontory with cliffs on three sides. There are wonderful views of bays, beaches and headlands, but the township is quite bare, including the trees which are stripped of their leaves by flocks of sulphur-crested and black cockatoos. These raucous-sounding birds rule the town from their lookouts on top of the telegraph wires.

But a mere day's drive east, so the hotel owner told me, at the foot of an escarpment, the land is lush and green and there are enormous lagoons full of pink swamp flowers surrounded by thick orchid-bearing jungles that the sun's rays never penetrate.

These wetlands contain more water birds than can be seen in any one place on earth; great herds of water buffalo; thousands of red and eastern grey kangaroos; brindle nail-tailed wallabies; wallaroos and enormous man-eating crocodiles. Apart from the crocodiles, I would enjoy seeing everything else.

The sea around Darwin is full of barramundi and other tropical fish and dotted with islands where the blacks are rumoured to live exactly as they did when Australia was visited by Captain Cook.

15 October 1919—Still Darwin

We have been shopping. Mr Fysh said that as we are famous in Darwin, we must look the part. I am now the proud owner of new pyjamas, trousers, two shirts, boots and my first pair of lace-up shoes.

George looks as flash as I do. He is pretending not to be pleased, but he is.

16 October 1919—News from the Defence Department

Mr McGinness telegraphed General Legge, the officer in charge of the survey, to say that although the Department of Defence and the Secretary of

State for the Colonies in London chose the Gulf route, mainly because of the ability to ship fuel and food supplies to the coastal towns, he and Mr Fysh did not recommend it. Instead, they suggested the Barkly Tablelands route mapped by Reginald Lloyd (with his motor bike and sidecar), because it is more direct and the area is known to be flat and treeless with only a small amount of scrub growing on the fringes.

General Legge telegraphed back instructing Mr McGinness, as leader of the surveying team, to return to Cloncurry along the Barkly Tablelands route and to build the airfields wherever he thought suitable, as fuel supplies could be brought in later by bullock wagon or packhorse.

The telegraph then mentioned that the first unofficial contestants, French Lieutenants Poulet and Benoist, had left Paris on 14 October, flying a twin-engine Caudron G-4 with two extra fuel tanks to increase flying range. It was General Legge's opinion they could arrive at any time.

The telegraph finished with the information that the race winners would not be flying into Sydney because that would mean their aircraft would have to cross the Blue Mountains twice. Instead they would fly straight down the middle of New South Wales to Melbourne.

I am so sorry, Matt. It means you will not be able

to see the winners in the flesh. I promise to tell you everything.

George, Billy and I are to go with Mr McGinness. We will travel through Pine Creek, Mataranka, Daly Waters, Newcastle Waters, Eva Downs, Creswell Downs, Anthony's Lagoon, Brunette Downs, Avon Downs and Camooweal.

George says he'll be glad when we are back in Longreach. He is worried about Mr McGinness's navigational skills. Until now Mr Fysh has done all the navigating, plus George isn't keen on building airstrips, he says it wasn't part of the deal.

Mr Fysh is happy about staying in Darwin to build the Darwin and Katherine airstrips, as he likes the Darwin social life. George says Mr Fysh means the crocodile hunting and the evening soirees held at the rich squatters' homes. He says Mr Fysh is a bit of a ladies' man, whereas McGinness just wants the whole business over and done with so he can get on with organising the finances for their aerial service.

George thinks getting money to start up the aerial service will be hard, as more than three quarters of Australia's population haven't seen an aircraft, unless it was on the black and white newsreels of the Great War.

Give Mama a big kiss and tell her not to work so hard.

Love, Jack.

17 October 1919—Fannie Bay

Dear Matt,

How wonderful to receive more letters.

Sorry that you have broken yet another of Mrs Wentworth's ornaments. How odd that you, who are so delicate when turning a screw or inserting a wire, are so clumsy when dusting.

I will answer all your questions tomorrow. Today I am going barramundi fishing at Fannie Bay.

Later

I didn't catch anything but George did, so we're having fried fish for tea.

18 October 1919—Buddhist Temple

We are to remain in the Victoria Hotel for another four or five days while Mr Fysh begins the building of the Darwin airstrip. The hotel owner doesn't mind Billy being in our room, he says that drovers don't like being parted from their dogs either.

At first the Darwin airstrip was to be built in the middle of the racecourse, but it has a depression in its centre and it is too short for a runway. Now it is to be built 2 miles north of the town near the Fannie Bay Gaol.

I passed Fannie Bay Gaol yesterday and peeked in through the corrugated tin fence. It appears to be only for blacks. George says they probably keep the whites in another part. The blacks looked truly miserable sitting in the dust. Nothing like the happy myalls we saw on our trip.

The airstrip labourers will be paid 4 shillings an hour and the job will cost 700 pounds, which a member of the Federal Government thinks is a wicked waste of public money. But the airstrip must be finished before the wet sets in, so the labourers can ask what they like.

The competition ends on 31 December. The wet season begins at the end of November and continues until March, during which time everything goes mouldy, especially leather. Mr Fysh says that the rain will make the spear grass on the strip grow as tall as a man, so he'll have to have it cut down just before the winners arrive. So far the worst obstructions to the making of the airfield are two banyan trees, two scrub-turkey's nests, and a rice paddy. The owner, a Mr Winston Chong, is not happy about moving.

There are a lot of market gardeners and gold miners from China living up here. Once there were more Orientals than white settlers. Now it's about fifty-fifty. They settled here after the South

Australian Government gave them permission because no-one else would.

You see, Matt, the Northern Territory used to be attached to South Australia. (Before that it was part of New South Wales. Can you imagine New South Wales stretching this far?) But when South Australia entered the Commonwealth of Australian states in 1910, the Northern Territory was left behind, so it is now ruled by an Administrator.

I can tell you for certain that this does not please the residents. They say it doesn't give them any say in the Commonwealth Government. You should hear the arguments that go on about it in the public bar of the Victoria Hotel.

The Chinamen's families live in falling-down banana-leaf shanties. The men wear half-mast trousers that look very strange, and pointed round straw hats and straw sandals that they make themselves. They carry huge weights tied to each end of a pole balanced on their shoulders. This is how they water their plants. George says it is amazing how much one small Oriental man can carry.

The children don't go to school and the families appear to have no money at all. But they have a fine temple. It is the most ornate building in Darwin. It is painted red and gold and has swinging lanterns, tall brass candlesticks (smelly burning sticks called incense), jangling bell music played by a bald-headed man wearing what looks like a yellow dressing-gown, and statues of ancestor gods and a scantily-dressed fat man called the Smiling Buddha.

I know all about it because Sing Lu, the twelve-year-old son of the hotel cook, took me there for three pennies. He put the pennies in a bowl and the man in the dressing-gown gave us green tea in a handleless cup. The man is a priest. He speaks no English. Sing Lu's English is good although he has only been in Australia a year and has never been to school.

Sing Lu works in the hotel. He cleans the floors with a broom and mop that are bigger than he is. He carries the slop buckets out of the kitchen; scrubs the huge cooking pots; empties the spittoons from the bar; replaces the wood used to heat the copper to boil the sheets and towels; dusts all the rooms; and empties the chamber pots.

He and his father send all their money back to China to his mother, who looks after Sing Lu's four sisters and their ancestors' graves. Ancestors' graves are very important. They must not be left unattended or their ancestors' ghosts will become lonely and may leave the graves in search of their living relations.

I asked Sing Lu how he thought the ghosts would find him and his father in Australia? He said the ghosts would attach themselves to a ship and come to Darwin that way. He truly believes this. I don't.

The strangest thing is the way they send their money back to China. They do not use the banks. They give their money, and directions of how to find their families, to a Mr Chang Lee, and he somehow gets the money back to China and to the right families. George said he wouldn't trust anyone with his money. But Sing Lu said that everyone trusts Chang Lee.

19 October 1919—Victoria Hotel

The Victoria Hotel is unusual for Darwin as it is built of stone. It is also infested with white ants (termites) that eat everything, including leather, so we put our boots on a stool in a tin bath overnight. When I lie down I can hear them munching.

There are many old-timers staying here, including pearlers from Broome, buffalo hunters from the Rum Jungle, prospectors from the Kimberleys, sandalwood-harvesters, and holidaying cattlemen. There is even a Mrs Wolfram Brown, who runs a mine worked by two hundred men from China, without another white person for hundreds of miles. She is a tough old chook I can tell you.

Each morning I take Billy for a walk along the seafront. Sometimes I see the troopers from Fannie Bay Gaol guarding the black prisoners who are building the road, but most of the time I talk to the black fishermen about how to catch Darwin's favourite fish, the barramundi.

While they fish, I teach Billy to fetch sticks, or we sit together on the rocks and I tell them about you, Mama, Pa, Sydney, Una Bloom, Lord Billy and Murdering Tommy. In return, they tell me how the stingray got his poisonous tail and other stories of their Dreamtime.

At first I didn't understand them but I have become used to their pidgin English. They are so generous with their knowledge, Matt. They have taught me how to keep a debbil-debbil out of our camp by drawing a circle around it, and how to protect my bare footprints from bad spirits that might cast evil spells over them. I must wear emu feather shoes so the spirit can't tell which direction I'm going in (emu feather shoes are good for tricking a tracker as well). They also taught me how to bake barramundi, wrapped in wild ginger, in a hole in the ground.

They give me fish to bring back to the hotel where Sing Lu's father cooks them for us. He won't use wild ginger; he uses a salty black sauce called soy sauce. It's nice if you don't pour too much on, but George doesn't think it will become popular. 'Chow tucka', as George calls it, will never take the place of baked potatoes, pumpkin and lamb chops.

In the late afternoon, once the heat has worn off and the water cart has sprayed the dust, everyone from our hotel plays cricket in the street. One time Mr Fysh hit a sixer into the sea which ended the game, so he had to shout everyone a beer.

At night, we watch magic lantern shows in the hotel lounge, play the pianola, or visit the theatre. Last night we went to see the American film *The Vagabond* with Charlie Chaplin. Before the film there was a live show with a magician, a boxing kangaroo, and a whip-cracker called Skiting Jimmy, who cracked two whips at once and whipped a cigarette out of his female partner's mouth from the other side of the stage.

We also play darts or cards in the bar. George doesn't mind me playing cards, as long as I don't bet money and don't drink beer. So I bet with match sticks and drink lemon squash.

20 October 1919—Still Darwin

Mr McGinness says I am not to be disappointed about not being here when the winners arrive. He says he is disappointed too, but that during our return trip he will teach me everything he knows about aeroplanes, and George and I can teach him everything we know about Model T Fords. George says he doesn't mind waiting to see the winners until after we are back in Longreach, not if it means getting home sooner.

Mr McGinness started my first aeroplane lesson today. Here it is. A BE2E has to have a team of two. This is because a BE2E engine is started by spinning its propeller by hand. But if a gunner is shot and the plane comes down, the pilot can start the engine by setting the throttle, lashing the joystick back to stop the aircraft's tail from lifting off the ground, getting out of the cockpit to swing the propeller, then quickly getting back into the cockpit before the aircraft takes off on its own.

Did you know that aeroplanes can fly upside down? One day Mr McGinness was performing a loop the loop, when out of the clouds came a German Albatross, firing straight at his BE2E. As they reached the top of the loop Mr Fysh shot down the Albatross. Isn't that amazing! I would love to do a loop the loop.

And the last bit of information is especially for you. The first Australian woman to fly was Florence Taylor, wife of George A Taylor. Mrs Taylor flew her husband's glider in 1909. A female pilot is called an aviatrix.

21 October 1919—Last day in Darwin

Everything is ready to go. I will be sorry to say goodbye to Mr Fysh, although I will see him in Longreach after the race is won.

I am also sorry to say goodbye to Sing Lu, who has become a very good cricketer due to my coaching.

I will post this today.

Love, Jack.

22 October 1919—Goodbye Darwin

Dear Matt,

Sorry if the writing is wriggly, I am writing this as we go along.

With a sparkling, revitalised Lizzie (which, once we hit the dusty road, wasn't sparkling for long) and our horn sounding like a sick cow, we waved goodbye to a saluting Mr Fysh, to the staff of the Victoria Hotel, and to everyone in the bar who came out onto the veranda to give us a cheer.

Once again the reporters were there to record our departure. Sing Lu gave me a present: a pair of ivory chopsticks in a long, thin black lacquered box with strange writing on it, and a new collar for Billy. George said they probably cost him his week's wages. I felt mean as I had not thought to buy him a present but I promised to send him a dictionary the minute I got back to Longreach.

It's 185 miles to Katherine, so we will have to camp along the way.

23 October 1919—Katherine

This morning we passed the turn-off to the gorge country (thirteen gorges in total). I would have loved to have seen them, but we kept going and arrived hot, dusty and thirsty in time for a hotel lunch at Katherine. Katherine is in the middle of a bout of tick fever, or redwater fever, which kills cattle, so the bar was full of worried cattlemen.

It is in Katherine that Mr Fysh will build the second airstrip for the air race competitors and for his and Mr McGinness's aerial service. But it will be some time before their aerial service uses the airstrip, as Mr Fysh and Mr McGinness intend starting up in western Queensland first.

24 October 1919—Katherine

I went to the Katherine telegraph office for news of the air race and discovered that the second contestants left England three days ago. They are Captain Mathews and Sergeant Kay, flying a Sopwith Wallaby. I asked Mr McGinness about the Sopwith Wallaby, and he drew me a picture.

We spent the day searching for tyres. Tyres are hard to find in the Northern Territory and we do not have enough spares with us if ours tear.

25 October 1919—Mataranka

We left Katherine at dawn. Once out of town, the track turned into a cattle pad leading straight to the tiny settlement of Mataranka, which is a blacks' camp situated beside the Elsey River.

As we drove through, I thought I recognised some of the men I had fished with in Darwin. George said the men most likely went walkabout to Darwin every few months to get a feed of saltwater fish. Imagine a walkabout of over 200 miles.

We stopped at the Old Elsey Station to fill up with water and to deliver a parcel to the owner's wife. It was dress material she had ordered months earlier. She was very happy to get it and made us a pot of tea and a plate of buttered scones, while her husband told us we were crazy driving east with the wet season so close.

26 October 1919—Daly Waters

Daly Waters is a pretty place, with a natural spring bubbling out of the ground surrounded by lush vegetation.

I spent an hour floating in the pool staring up the ragged skirts of the Cocos palms while Lizzie cooled down. Billy proved to be a very good swimmer although he preferred to lie on my stomach as I floated.

Daly Waters is roughly 400 miles south of Darwin. It was named by the explorer John McDouall Sturt (the one who named Sturt's desert pea) when he passed through in 1861 on his third effort to cross Australia. There is a tree with a big 'S' carved into its trunk to show he was here.

I told George that we should carve a 'G' and a 'J' on a tree somewhere along our track. Then I added a 'B' for Billy.

Daly Waters is a tiny settlement built around the Darwin to Adelaide telegraph line. Here are two interesting things I found out about the telegraph line. One was that it was built in pieces so, for a time, a pony express rider had to ride the 300 mile gap between Daly Waters and Tennant Creek, which is further south, to deliver the important overseas telegraph messages. These were then telegraphed on to Adelaide. Fancy being a pony express rider. How exciting!

The second thing is that twice a year, the Daly Waters' telegraphist rides 266 miles north to meet the Roper River supply boat, which brings his stores and ammunition all the way from Adelaide around the east coast, sailing halfway around Australia's coastline.

George is not happy with Lizzie's back left tyre and Mr McGinness is not happy with having to do so much paperwork. He says he does not have Mr Fysh's artistic ability. Even so, his maps are easy to read, which is the most important thing, as the air race competitors will need to read them when they use this route to reach Longreach from Darwin.

29 October 1919—Newcastle Waters Cattle Station

It has been two days since I wrote. This route is not as difficult as the Gulf Track, but we are driving at such a rattling pace that I don't have the time or energy to sit and write.

We have stopped off at the Newcastle Waters Cattle Station on our way to Newcastle Waters. The owner, Mr Lewis, made us most welcome. He and his wife have had no visitors for over six months and he said he was feeling like a good yarn.

Over a pot of the strongest black tea I have ever drunk, Mr Lewis explained how the Mudbarra blacks guided the first mob of cattle all the way from the Katherine overland telegraph line to Newcastle Waters. He also warned us of how inadequate the Northern Territory stock routes were (these are the ones we will be following), especially the Marranji Track, which has a reputation of being the most hazardous and treacherous stock route in the whole of Australia.

This news sobered George and Mr McGinness considerably.

Mr Lewis said he would be pleased when Syd Peacock finished the thirteen bores he'd been contracted to build between Yellow Waterhole and Anthony's Lagoon. He said we must watch out for Syd. His camp would be easy to see as it consisted of six horse-drawn wagons and a steam engine which Syd used to bore the holes into the earth.

I immediately thought of a railway engine. But George says it is different type of steam engine.

Mrs Lewis told me that the Murranji Track is named after the Murranji frog which can live underground for years without water. 'Just as well,' she added, 'there's been precious little rain out here lately.'

I am so tired I am off to bed.

30 October 1919—Newcastle Waters

We left the cattle station early and arrived at the tiny township of Newcastle Waters in the afternoon, with only two punctures on the way. Mr McGinness and George have a bet on how many punctures we will have before we reach Cloncurry.

No sooner had we unpacked Lizzie beside the Newcastle Waters telegraph station than Mr McGinness was off looking for labourers to build the airstrip on the first bit of flat land he could find. As there were no settlers around and the black men wouldn't work, he employed their wives, who immediately started clearing away the trees, rocks and long grass, while their lazy husbands looked on, laughing.

The women's payment will be two bags of flour, twenty yards of Turkey-red material, twenty-four sticks of tobacco, and photographs of themselves, developed in Longreach and delivered by the trader who brings in the goods for the only store in Newcastle Waters. This store is owned by George Man Fong, who said he knew Sing Lu and his father.

George said he bet the men would smoke their wives' tobacco, use the material for their corroboree lap-laps, and stick the photographs in their hair for decoration.

Last night, as I lay under the tarpaulin, I could hear the *click, click* of boomerangs, the soft hum of the bullroarers, and the hypnotic chanting of voices coming from their camp. I think they were very happy to have the unexpected tobacco. The plant they normally smoke is called *pituri.* It is used to dull pain and hunger. George has tried it. He says it didn't taste right and gave him bad dreams.

3 November 1919—Murranji Track

It took three and a half days to finish the Newcastle Waters airstrip. This morning it was recorded and photographed, and after waving goodbye to the blacks, we set off east along the Murranji Track. Our map indicates that this track is 150 miles long and without water.

4 November 1919—Devil-devil country

The Murranji Track is the driest stretch of our whole journey. The blacks call it devil-devil country because of the dust devils that rise up, swirl around at great speed, then race across the plain to die, just as suddenly, as if dropped by a rifle shot. George says the dust devils are spirits who stop at their tribal boundaries.

It is a frightening place. Everywhere we look there are flocks of dead finches lying on the sand. A man or pup could die of thirst within eighteen hours out here. I keep giving Billy spoonfuls of water. But first I must blow on it to cool it, as the water in my water bottle is as warm as bathwater.

5 November 1919—Thirsty

We are having to ration the water, especially as Lizzie's radiator is steaming. Billy's little tongue is stuck out and he is panting all the time.

George thinks there are some secret wells and food stashes out here but that we would never find them. If we did, we wouldn't be able to touch them, as only those of the same totem can eat or drink from them.

Five punctures today.

6 November 1919—Still thirsty

Everything is the same as the last three days: hot, dusty and thirsty. This is such a desolate place.

The track we are following is so full of gilgai

holes that Mr McGinness and I must walk in front of Lizzie and fill them in. While I am doing this, Billy sits on the front seat beside George, as the earth is too hot for his feet. He is a very good automobile dog.

7 November 1919—Beetaloo

The drive from Newcastle Waters to Beetaloo seemed to take forever, even though we drove from dawn to dark for four days, all the time thinking that if we ran out of water we would die.

At Beetaloo we met a boundary rider and rabbit fencer called Harry Bathern, his black wife and their eight children.

Their one-room hut, which is dug into the ground to escape the wind, has no windows, no door and a roof made of flattened fuel drums. The inside walls are wallpapered with old *Bulletin* newspapers, the furniture is made from packing cases, and the mattresses are made from sugarbags stuffed with dry grass. Hanging from the rafters are hundreds of strips of sticky Boomerang flypaper and golden syrup-dabbed newspaper, with thousands of dead flies glued to their sticky surfaces. The pieces of paper are coated in orange dust and from a distance they look like Christmas decorations. But in truth, they are a giant fly cemetery.

The boundary rider refused to talk to us but his wife brought us fresh water and a skinned rabbit from her Coolgardie meat safe. Her children brought us knobbly cucumber-looking fruit, called *alungua,* and quandong fruit. George said they must have walked miles to find them in this barren place.

The eight children are as timid as possums. But after Mr McGinness let them sit in Lizzie, they became as chatty as a flock of galahs.

They called their father a 'combo', which is the word for a white man with a black wife. They said he never spoke to settlers or drovers, but that he spoke their mother's language and four other tribal languages.

George asked Mr McGinness how he thought his aerial service would help isolated outback families like this, and Mr McGinness said that it wouldn't at first, but with newly invented aircraft, and more of them, perhaps more people would settle the outback.

Mr McGinness's answer didn't please George. George thinks the outback isn't meant to be settled. I asked Mr McGinness how much these new aircraft would cost.

'A lot,' he said. 'Fysh and I will be lucky if we

can afford one already-shot-at Great War aircraft let alone anything newly invented.'

Later on George told me that Mr Fysh and Mr McGinness were dead broke. He couldn't see how they were going to raise enough money to start anything.

8 November 1919—Eva Downs

I almost lost Billy at Beetaloo. One of the littlest children took a liking to him and when it was time to leave, neither the child nor Billy could be found.

George went for a yabba (as he calls it) with the children's father. The man took flight, but within seconds, a tearful toddler handed back a tail-wagging, kangaroo-greased Billy. Which accounts for the grease spots on this page.

After Beetaloo, we drove over such a parched plain that when we chugged into Eva Downs, Lizzie's radiator was puffing like Syd Peacock's steam engine must puff when he is drilling. No, we have not seen Syd Peacock. Neither has the owner of Eva Downs who gave us the last dregs of his fresh water to keep us going. He said he would make do on bore water.

Bore water isn't good for radiators, it is too salty and too hot. (The Eva Downs bore is near boiling when it spurts out of its bore hole.)

Eva Downs' owner said that Syd Peacock's bores, along with the other thousand bores already pumping out water nonstop, are only a temporary measure for the lack of water.

He said no-one thinks that the Great Artesian Basin, which lies beneath one fifth of Australia, will ever empty, but it stands to reason that it has to one day. He reckons he can see a future when the bores dribble out their last drop.

'That's when I pack it in,' he said.

11 November 1919—Anthony's Lagoon

The last few days have been so exhausting, I have not felt like writing. In fact I feel as if I have been boiled alive.

The Eva Downs fresh water lasted Lizzie the two days it took us to reach Creswell Creek where we are now camped beside Anthony's Lagoon, famous for death adders' nests and giant goannas.

We didn't see any death adders, and if we had I don't think we'd have cared. We were so hot on arrival that we dipped our heads in the lagoon and drank until we nearly burst. Then we threw ourselves into the lagoon for a swim. With this heat, which dries your skin until it cracks like old leather, George and I have overcome our aversion to swimming, especially as there are no crocodiles this far inland.

George says that September to November is when the death adders are at their most venomous, but as there are no paper-like skins lying around, he reckons they are still hibernating or the big rock goannas have nosed them out and eaten them.

'So where are these big rock goannas?' I asked.

Because let me tell you, Matt, if I had a choice between death adders and giant goannas, I would choose death adders.

Giant goannas, as long as a man's arm and as agressive as a mad bull, are a frightening sight when they rear up on their four bow-legged legs and flick out their strange blue tongues. They remind me of the descriptions Lord Billy gave of his big animals. Imagine confronting a goanna twice the size of Lizzie. It's a frightening thought.

'Ahhh,' answered George, who had no idea of what I was thinking. 'The blacks have probably hunted them and eaten them. They love to feast on fattened rock goanna, and they use the oil from goanna skins to cure just about everything.'

See what I mean about everything eating everything up here?

With no fattened goannas around, we were dining on salt beef, damper and mouldy potatoes, when we were joined by a bounty hunter and his two blue heeler dogs. He introduced himself as Fred Cragg of the Barkly Tablelands. He said we were the first white men he'd seen in four months. He also said he'd learnt to read from tinned food labels and that he was hunting for wild goats and dingoes. Goats, because they pull up the roots of everything, and dingoes, because they attacked the calves.

Mr McGinness asked him if he didn't mind working on his own. Fred looked puzzled, then answered that he wasn't on his own; he had his horse and his dogs. But he did miss being able to buy proper tobacco.

It was a big hint, as he was staring at George's pipe when he said it, so George gave him a packet of Capstan Plus. In return, Mr Cragg unrolled a pile of cured goat skins and gave George a beautiful black and white hide.

12 November 1919—Still Anthony's Lagoon

We were woken this morning by the chuckling of a blue-winged kookaburra, the first I've heard for months. Did you know that in the dry season, instead of the young kookaburras flying off and finding themselves a mate, making a nest and laying eggs, they help feed the next batch of hatched eggs until the drought is over? Who would have thought a bird would know to do that.

Mr Cragg has gone. Mr McGinness said we should be gone too. He is in a hurry to reach Brunswick Downs. He says the sooner he finishes the Defence Department's airstrip building job, the sooner he can get started on finding investors for his and Mr Fysh's aerial service. Part of the time, he says, this should be easy, as blind Freddy can see the benefit of flying. The other part of the time he thinks could be hard, because the men with the money might be too old-fashioned to invest in flying.

14 November 1919—Solid rubber tyres

We've had a couple of bad days. Lizzie's clutch plates began slipping so badly that George had to hack his new boot to pieces to make a leather friction pad to stop it. He wasn't happy about it as he loved those new boots. Next, we got bogged and had to dig Lizzie out. Then we got a puncture.

George is sick of mending inner tubes; he says he can't understand why they don't make a solid rubber tyre. Mr McGinness says it's the same with aircraft tyres; that if an aircraft's tyre blows out while it is landing or taking off, it can cause the aircraft to flip over. Both men agreed that it would cost a small fortune to make solid tyres.

15 November 1919—Brunette Downs

We arrived at Brunette Downs yesterday and started working on the airstrip. We built it ourselves, near a large billabong called Helen Springs Lake.

The Barkly Tablelands are 4,000 feet above sea level, which makes it cold in the mornings and evenings, but the land is billiard-table flat, so all George and I had to do was remove a few stones while Mr McGinness marked it down on his survey map and took some photographs. He does not take cinemagraphic photos because sand got into the camera long ago and jammed it.

Now we are having a cup of tea, and although it is late in the afternoon, we are setting off for Avon Downs. Mr McGinness says we will camp on the way.

17 November 1919—Linda Downs

We passed through Avon Downs early yesterday, travelled all day, and we are now camped beside Linda Downs homestead. Here we met the famous Mr Eberneezer Benjamin, doctor, dentist, optometrist, water diviner and jack-of-all-trades.

Mr Benjamin travels around in a covered wagon full of medicines and essentials, such as ribbons, jewellery, shoes, boots, drapery, china, cutlery, parasols, fans, the latest sheet music, romance novels, pocketknives, tinware, stationery, whips, bridles, stockmen's leggings, nails, lamps and groceries. His wagon is pulled by two broken-in brumbies, with two more tied behind. A sign on each side of the wagon says: 'For a small fee, Mr Benjamin will cure all ills'.

'I have been called upon to mend a fractured jaw; stitch up a woman after a caesarean birth; remove a gangrenous leg; pull teeth, human, horse and dog; and divine for water,' he announced grandly.

'How did you mend the fractured jaw?' asked the owner of Linda Downs, fingering his decidedly crooked jaw.

Mr Benjamin pushed up his sleeves to reveal amazingly white shirt cuffs (amazing because of the dust surrounding us) and with long expressive fingers showed us exactly how he'd wired up the jaw with fuse wire.

'And how did you stitch up the woman after her caesarean operation?' asked George, winking at me to show he thought Mr Benjamin to be an enormous liar.

'With kangaroo-tail tendon sutures, dipped in whiskey for the inside and dipped in iodine for the outside. A smear of kerosene to kill any germs, and a liberal smear of fat to minimise scarring.'

'And how do you find water?' asked Mr Fysh.

Mr Benjamin tapped his nose. 'I smell it, sir. Although I also carry a diviner's wand. Mainly for show, you understand. But the truth is, it's all in the nose.'

'Then you're not a rainmaker,' said George, thinking to trick Mr Benjamin.

'I am not, sir. Although I have seen it done. I have seen it rain so hard that small fish fall from the sky and swim around in pools and gutters, hundreds of miles from a river or coastline.'

He sighed heavily. 'I wish I could do it. But haven't found a black gentleman who will teach me. No sir, my gift is the ability to smell water underground.'

'Can you smell any around here,' asked the owner.

'Not underground.' Then he pointed to a large

dead tree in the distance. 'But there is water in that tree.'

'Can you smell it from here?' I asked, full of amazement.

'No, dear lad, I can't. But one can always be sure of water in a hollow tree. All you need is an axe to chop off the top and there it is.'

After this piece of bush wisdom, he asked if anyone needed his services, while assuring us that his were 'the best of European potions'.

On finding none of us sick, he left us and was soon asleep in the back of his wagon.

19 November 1919—Camooweal

After driving for two days, we crossed over the Northern Territory border and, 5 miles later, arrived at Camooweal, the most westerly town in Queensland, just in time for breakfast. We were all exuberant as we had successfully crossed the Barkly Tablelands two days faster than Mr McGinness had calculated.

Camooweal is suffering a blowfly plague. They get under our fly nets and into our eyes and mouths. We have resorted to dabbing ourselves with kerosene in the hope of keeping them off our faces.

It is through Camooweal that the drovers bring

their mobs of cattle, a thousand head at a time (hence the blowflies), overlanding them down the Georgina River and, sometimes, all the way to South Australia.

It is an immense trip, and I am full of admiration for them, but I would not wish to do it. It seems to me, the more Mr McGinness talks about the ease of flying, the more it makes sense to me that to be up in the air, away from the dust (and the blowflies), is infinitely more desirable. Not to mention the adventure of a lifetime. The earth must look so amazing from up there.

We stopped off at Freckleton's store to stock up with stores, as ours were running dangerously low, and to find out how aircraft fuel supplies can be delivered, how long it will take, and how the 4-gallon drums will be hoisted level with the aircraft's engine so that the 20,000 gallons can be pumped into its fuel tanks.

The storekeeper said it could all be done for an agreed price, then he asked us if we'd heard the latest news about the air race. Which of course we hadn't because we'd been in the desert.

'Then you wouldn't know that the French are in the lead,' he said.

'They aren't in the race,' growled George. 'They're not Australian.'

'True,' agreed the storekeeper, 'but they're

racing anyway, and they are well ahead of the third contestants, Captain Ross Smith, Lieutenant Keith Smith and Sergeants Bennett and Shiers who are in a Vickers Vimy aircraft called "God help us all".'

George grunted in disgust at this piece of news, but I thought it exciting.

'Then there are those poor blighters, Lieutenants Douglas and Rose, whose Alliance P2 Seabird biplane crashed three minutes after taking off, with no survivors,' continued the storekeeper.

This last piece of news sobered me up. It's one thing to dream about how wonderful flying would be, and I do dream about it, Matt, but quite another to think of crashing and dying.

I will not be posting this letter to you from here. Camooweal is 400 miles to the east of Newcastle Waters, 400 miles to the west of Cloncurry, and 500 miles to the south of Borroloola. Borroloola is where Camooweal gets its mail and supplies from, so I would be back in Longreach before you received it.

I forgot to tell you. I am learning to drive Lizzie. But only because Mr Fysh is not here and only when George and Mr McGinness need to do the pushing. I already knew the left pedal is the brake, the middle pedal is reverse and the third pedal, when pushed to the floor, disengages the clutch and allows me to choose one of two speeds. But guiding the steering wheel is harder than it looks.

The problem is that I am not tall enough to reach the pedals and see through the windscreen at the same time, so I have to sit on my rolled-up swag, and touch the floor pedals with my toes.

Mr McGinness assures me that flying an aircraft is much easier than driving an automobile because it doesn't matter how short you are.

21 November 1919—Between Carlton Hills and Quamby

It took two days, working from dawn to dusk, for George and me to clear the Camooweal airstrip. Mr McGinness made a map and took photographs, and then we were off, leaving blowfly land behind us just as the sun was setting. George thought it a stupid time to set off, but Mr McGinness said every hour counts.

Now we are camped somewhere between the Carlton Hills and Quamby. Earlier in the day we caught up with and passed a mob of sheep being driven to the Cloncurry railhead. There was a boss drover, two ringers, two musterers, a cook in a wagonette packed high with food, water and sleeping rolls, a mob of horses, and a dozen sheep dogs that bounded effortlessly over the sheep's backs to snap and growl at the stragglers.

It took all my strength to hold Billy, who wriggled and barked at the other dogs. I had no idea he had drover-dog blood in him.

The cook asked if we wanted a cuppa, as he was setting up for morning tea, so we stopped for a rest.

I asked the cook why there were so many horses and dogs.

He said that each rider needed five day horses, one night horse, and three sheep dogs. He preferred a good mongrel himself, but the boss preferred black and white kelpies.

'With my bitzer,' he boasted, 'I've driven sheep from Cape York to Launceston and didn't lose a one.'

'What about Bass Strait?' asked one of the ringers, who'd heard this yarn before.

'We didn't go that way,' said the cook. Then with his face as straight as a poker he turned to me and asked me how much I wanted for Billy.

George shouted, 'Ten quid.'

I said he was not for sale.

24 November 1919—Cloncurry

I has taken us three days to get here but only because the track was in good condition, which means flat, flat, flat.

I never thought I would be pleased to see

Cloncurry's rusting copper furnaces, corrugated iron shanties, tattered tents, and the cemetery, ever again, but I am.

Mr McGinness unpacked all his belongings and settled into the Post Office Hotel from where he is going to oversee the building of the Cloncurry airstrip, then wait to congratulate the winners of the air race.

The hotel owner showed us some old newspapers, which mentioned Captain Smith's and Lieutenant Smith's departure from Hounslow, London. The newspaper said that the weather was foggy and unfit for flying, but the intrepid brothers and their two engineers took off anyway, taking rations of sandwiches, tinned meat, biscuits, chocolate, and Bovril. But it was so cold in the unheated aircraft, the sandwiches froze solid, and a mere three hours after take off, the pilots were forced to land at Rouanne, France.

There was also a paragraph on the fifth contestants, Captain Wilkins and Lieutenants Williams, Rendle and Potts, who have taken off in a Blackburn Kangaroo biplane.

It is so exciting to imagine all these aircraft flying over France, Italy, Crete, Egypt, Arabia, Persia, India, Thailand, Singapore, Timor and even more exotic unknown places if they have to make an unscheduled stop.

The next bit of news about the air race came from the post office telegraph man, who gets the information first-hand from overseas.

He had three stories about the Smith brothers, who he said were his favourites to win. The first was when the Smith brothers' Vickers Vimy became bogged in Pisa, Italy. Sergeant Bennett had to hold down the aircraft's tail to stop it nose diving into the mud, while Captain Smith revved the engine as hard as he could. Then, as the aircraft moved forward, Sergeant Bennett had to run alongside it and grab hold of Sergeant Shier's hand. He managed to vault into his cockpit just as the aircraft rose into the air.

In the second story, the Smith brothers were forced to land near Baghdad. The winds were so high, the aircraft would have blown away had it not been for fifty Indian soldiers holding it down.

The third story was when, after crossing the mighty Himalayan mountains in fog and sleet and arriving safely in Calcutta, the Smith brothers discovered that the Frenchmen were only two hours ahead. In an attempt to catch up, they took off as soon as their aircraft was ready. But as they flew over Calcutta, two hawks flew into their propeller, almost causing them to crash.

The telegraph man said that the Frenchmen were still in the lead, and that they or the Smith brothers were expected to arrive in Darwin in sixteen days or less, and in Cloncurry four days later.

Oh Matt, doesn't it sound wonderfully exciting? Doesn't it make your blood race just thinking of those two aircraft neck to neck, or propeller to propeller? It does mine. I wish I was a pilot flying in the air race.

Later

On hearing how close the aircraft were, Mr McGinness sent George and I off to Schaeffe Street to buy some picks and shovels.

The shopkeeper remembered us from when he had tried to sell us picks and shovels to go gold prospecting. He said I'd grown a treat and demanded to hear all our news. He was all ears until George mentioned that we had driven through Camooweal. At this, he butted in to ask if we knew that Burke and Wills might have reached Camooweal.

'That's how Camooweal got started. And did you know that Burke named Cloncurry after his cousin, Lady Elizabeth Cloncurry?'

Twenty minutes later, after he had told us all he knew about Burke and Wills, he sold us ten shovels and ten picks. Outside his shop George said he had Burke and Wills on the brain.

Back at the hotel we found Mr McGinness in the bar reminding the out-of-work copper miners of the deal they'd made with him back in August.

'Still on about building that airstrip,' laughed one man. 'Thought you'd have got over that nonsense by now. Ridgy-didge, mate! You're flogging a dead horse with that idea.'

Mr McGinness didn't get annoyed. He just stated how much the Government would pay and how their names would be listed in *The Cloncurry Advocate* when the winners of the air race arrived, which could be in about twelve days. Before you could snap your fingers, he had a queue of men clamouring for him to put their names down on his sheet of paper.

George was angry at that. We had not been paid extra to build the three airstrips we've cleared nor was it likely that our names will be featured in the Longreach newspaper.

Posting this huge letter today.

Love, Jack.

25 November 1919—Still in Cloncurry

Dear Matt,

I have received a letter from you, sent on from somewhere. It is very old and stained. I am very excited to hear that you went to Richmond to see the open day of the New South Wales Government Aviation School.

George and I are getting ready to leave for Longreach, as Mr McGinness doesn't need us any more.

While packing away our food for the next few days, I found an old newspaper wrapped around the onions. In it was an article about the air race. This is what it said.

After leaving England on 21 October, the second contestants, Captain Mathews and Sergeant Kay, flying a single engine Sopwith Wallaby, became snowbound in Germany. Captain Mathews has been entrusted with a letter from His Majesty King Edward to the Governor-General of the Commonwealth of Australia. George says if he doesn't manage to dig his aircraft out of the snow, the letter might never make it. George is not a Royalist.

There was also more about the Frenchmen, who seem to have caught the imagination of the world.

While crossing Persia, they were forced to land in the desert where they were harassed by hostile nomads trying to set fire to their aircraft.

And there's been a second fatal accident. The sixth contestants, Captain Howell and Lieutenant

Fraser, crashed their Martinsyde Type A, Mark I into the Adriatic Sea. The whole crew drowned.

It's all old news, but it was both exciting and sad.

I forgot to tell you, George won the bet on how many punctures Lizzie got. Mr McGinness was out by thirty-five.

I will post this before we leave.

Love, Jack.

30 November 1919—End of the round trip

Dear Matt,

After a gruelling six days of punctures, dry creek beds, and George's driving (except when he had to push and I had to drive), we have arrived back in Longreach. How welcome the long main street looked.

Lizzie has travelled 2,229 miles, and George says she needs a good rest. She is parked at the back of Longreach Motor Company. Billy and I are back at Mrs Banks's hostel, although Mrs Banks is not keen on Billy staying.

Of course, the first thing I did was ask for any news of the air race.

Avery told me that Captain Mathews and

Sergeant Kay had just arrived in Vienna, Austria. He also said the Smith brothers had caught up with the Frenchmen in Burma. The crews swapped adventure stories before the Frenchmen took off again, still in the lead.

Then, when the Smith brothers were coming in to land on the Malay Peninsula, they saw that the airstrip was not safe, because although the natives had chopped down the trees, they had not removed the stumps. As it was too late to pull out of the landing, Captain Smith attempted to swerve around the stumps, but he hit one and the Vickers Vimy's tail skid broke. They were not carrying a spare tail skid so a new one had to be made, which meant they lost a day.

1 December 1919—Longreach

It's an odd feeling being back in Longreach. Stranger still to have the expedition over and done with. I miss listening to the men talking. I miss Lizzie and sleeping under her. I miss the adventure of never knowing what is coming next. Some people say the outback is monotonous, but I don't think so. Even making the fire a dozen times a day, and pushing Lizzie out of creek beds was exciting.

It's hard getting up at 7 am, washing my head

under the cold water tap, and having to run the three blocks to the Longreach Motor Company so I won't be late, because one of the boys has hidden my boots. Which they do for a joke.

It's even harder going back to being an apprentice of no importance, with a dozen men bossing me about.

George says he feels odd about being back as well, sort of deflated, but I think he is truly glad to be sitting in his comfortable smoking spot in the sun outside the motor room. He did say he missed Mr Fysh and Mr McGinness going on all the time about their aerial service. It was only when he said it that I realised that was what I missed the most too.

There are so many questions I want to ask Mr McGinness. Such as, how many maps would the contestants have to carry? Would the contestants' aircraft engines be worn out after flying 11,500 miles? Would refuelling be a problem in countries that don't have automobiles or fuel? And how would the pilots make themselves understood if they were forced to land in a country that didn't speak English?

2 December 1919—Longreach Motor Company

I've just come from the newsagents, where I picked up *The Bulletin,* and from the post office, where I picked up your and Mama's letters.

The Bulletin says, in large letters, that Poulet and Benoist have abandoned the race after discovering a cracked cylinder in their engine. Then, in smaller print, it says that Captain Mathews and Sergeant Kay (the 'King's messengers', as George calls them) have left Thailand and are flying towards the Dutch East Indies. Then, in even smaller letters, that Captain Wilkins and Lieutenants Williams, Rendle and Potts have crashed their Blackburn Kangaroo into a Cretan lunatic asylum, fortunately with no casualties. I have cut it all out for my scrapbook.

Now to your letter and your long list of questions. Yes, Avery hasn't stopped badgering me about our trip since I set foot in the hostel. When I am tired of talking about it, he hits me with a pillow. He says I have grown conceited because I am the first boy to have driven across the top of Australia. I haven't, I promise.

Greg and Paul have returned home to the Georgina River country, so Avery and I have the room to ourselves. We have great pillow fights, which sets Billy off barking like crazy, then Mrs

Banks knows he is inside and she hits the roof. She is very, very unhappy about Billy.

Avery has made me promise to go with him to see the winners arrive in Longreach, and to introduce him to Mr Fysh and Mr McGinness. He is also keeping a scrapbook on the race contestants' progress.

Yes, I am glad to be back at Longreach Motor Company, although it is hotter under the tin roof than it was in the Gulf of Carpentaria, and I am glad to be getting on with my apprenticeship after four months of gallivanting around, as Mrs Banks calls it. But, oh Matt, it seems so unadventurous.

Lord Billy is in town. He is staying with his family out in a shanty beside the Chinatown. George took me and Billy out to see him. We went on his motorbike. Lord Billy greeted me like a long lost son and was flattered that I'd named Billy after him.

Must go, Mrs Banks is calling for me to tie Billy up as he is digging up her garden. She insists he stay outside. But he sneaks in through the wire-screen door. I don't want to tie him up. It seems cruel to restrict his freedom when he had the whole of Northern Australia to play in.

Posting this today.

Love, Jack.

3 December 1919—Longreach

Dear Matt,

It has been so hot today that the water truck has been past four times spraying the roads to lay the dust, but it still gets down my throat and makes me cough. I wonder if an aircraft can fly through dust. I asked George if dust could make an aircraft's engine stall. He said he didn't know and to stop asking him questions about machines that haven't the good sense to remain on the ground.

The winners are getting closer every day. I wonder if I will get to meet them? George says we ought to after all the work we did on the airstrips.

Avery and I have made Billy a fine kennel which he hates. He looks so sad tied up outside of it that I sneak him in at night. Avery says he won't tell. He has also helped me pick out a dictionary and a leather belt to send to Sing Lu. Avery is a good mate. I hope you meet him some day.

4 December 1919—Betting

Each hotel has a bookie, and the betting on the air race is becoming frantic.

What with the news of Captain Wilkins's Blackburn Kangaroo crash-landing in Crete and the

Frenchmen dropping out, there has been a lot of money lost. Now they are betting on the minute the winners will set foot on Australian soil. Mrs Banks says it's disgusting the amount of money going into the bookies' bags.

Avery said if he was old enough to bet, he would have bet on Mr Kingsford Smith, piloting his two-engine Blackburn biplane with the latest Rolls Royce 126 KW engines. Only Kingsford Smith wasn't allowed to enter the race because Prime Minister Billy Hughes said his navigator wasn't qualified (even though he had flown all through the Great War), so Avery is barracking for the Smith brothers.

Mrs Banks said that if her religion allowed her to bet, which it doesn't; and if he was an Australian, which he isn't; and if he was still in the race, which he's not—she would bet on Lieutenant Etienne Poulet, because his name sounds romantic and he is such a gentleman.

'Gentleman my eye! He's an illegal entrant and a frog,' exclaimed George. George calls all French people frogs.

But Mrs Banks told me that Poulet, who paid for his own plane and fuel, had announced that, should he win a prize, he would donate it to the widow and four children of a French pilot killed while flying to Rome. 'That sounds like a gentleman to me,' she said.

Today I cut out a wonderful article from a magazine. It was about the Smith brothers being greeted in India by a Maharajah on an elephant, and about when they landed in Singapore. Apparently, the Singaporean airstrip, which was the Farrer Park Race Course, was too short, so Sergeant Bennett had to climb out of his cockpit and inch his way along the bouncing fuselage of the Vickers Vimy to weigh it down and help stop it. It halted an arm's length from the curving fence, with Sergeant Bennett clinging to its tail.

I think I will barrack for Sergeant Bennett. I think he is a daredevil and a hero.

5 December 1919—The Argus

Billy is tied outside. He weed on Mrs Banks's lounge mat and he is in Coventry.

I read in the Saturday *Argus* newspaper that in the United States of America, thirty-one of the first forty pilots died in aircraft crashes. I hope Mr McGinness and Mr Fysh, who I know has only landed a plane once, do not die this way, and I hope no more of the air race contestants crash.

The Argus also quoted Lieutenant Smith as having said that the flight between Burma and Thailand was far worse than any flight they had done during the war, as they had expected to be forced to land on top of a forest of trees at any moment.

I would like to know what preparations a pilot makes when they are about to land on top of trees, but George has forbidden me to mention the crashing of aircraft to Mr Fysh or Mr McGinness. Not that I could, Mr Fysh is still in Darwin and Mr McGinness is still in Cloncurry.

6 December 1919—Death charms

Last night Avery and I rode our bikes to shantytown to visit Lord Billy. But something was up.

The women were in their humpies, keening the way they do when a baby dies. The men were talking out back in the scrub. Some were wearing war paint (red ochre marks painted on their foreheads and chests). The boys who we normally talk to said that Lord Billy had gone walkabout.

They took us to our favourite tree where we sat in the branches, watching the blue grass-rats scuttling through the grass, while they explained what was going on.

A man had killed another man because he had stolen his wife. But as the taking of the law into his own hands without first discussing it with the

Elders is not allowed, the Elders were considering his punishment.

'Where's the man now,' I asked.

'Gone,' whispered one of the boys. 'But Elders make him come back. They already sent smoke signals and message sticks to the other tribes to watch out for him.'

'If he keeps running, how will they make him come back?' whispered Avery.

'They send a medicine man, who puts death charms on the paths that he walks and on the trees he walks under. Once he sees them, he come back plenty quick or he die plenty quick.'

We sat for a while watching the Elders talk. Then I asked the boys what they thought about men flying in aircraft high up in the air like eagles, and they laughed and said, 'They find that bad man, pretty quick from up there, eh?'

I'm not sure they know what an aircraft is. Most of them can't read so I suppose they aren't interested in newspapers.

7 December 1919—Batavia

Two or three days to go before we can expect the winners to arrive in Darwin. The Smith brothers' aircraft has already landed in Batavia, the capital of the Dutch East Indies. Apparently the Dutch Governor ordered two airfields to be built. George says the Dutch order the Javanese around like slaves.

From Batavia the Smith brothers will fly to Surabaya, Timor, then Australia! Yippee!

8 December 1919—Shantytown

Avery and I rode out to Lord Billy's camp again to find out what happened to the man the Elders put the death charm on.

Lord Billy was back with some big animal bones to sell. He said the man was still running and that it could take months to catch him. Then he taught us how to tell the difference between rodent and marsupial tracks, and showed us how the trackers would track the murderer. He also taught us to listen for the cries of the brown hawk, which he calls a telltale because these birds listen to women's gossip. Lord Billy says if you can understand the brown hawk, he will tell you where people are and what's going on.

'Like this morning,' he said, winking at me, 'a brown hawk whisper to me that the Smith brothers land him aircraft at Surabaya. Big rains mash up the earth at Surabaya, so aircraft sink in the mud for seven hours, not good for race, eh? Then the native people, like me, lend him bamboo sleeping mat and house mat to cover the mud and they take off again.'

Avery was very impressed, but George told me that Lord Billy can read, so I bet he's been reading *The Bulletin*.

Give Mama a big kiss and Pa a big hug, and a big hug for yourself.

Love, Jack.

9 December 1919—Arriving soon

Dear Matt,

The newspapers, which I am sure you are following just as closely as I am, say the Smith brothers have left Timor and will arrive in Darwin tomorrow. This is the longest part of the flight.

The first part of Australia they will see will be Bathurst Island's lighthouse and the HMAS Sydney, which has been ordered to cruise Torres Strait in case their aircraft crashes into the sea.

I wish I could see them come roaring over the horizon. I wish I was there instead of listening with my ear glued to the wireless like everyone else.

10 December 1919—The winners

Captain Smith, Lieutenant Smith, and Sergeants Shiers and Bennett have arrived at last.

At 3.40 pm, they were spotted flying out of the Timor Sea and over Bathurst Island. Then, with the help of smoke to show which way the wind was blowing, and a sheet to show them where the airstrip was, they landed at Fannie Bay. At the same time, a whole continent away, the Adelaide Town Hall bells spread the news to the Adelaide people that two of their sons had won the London to Darwin air race. The first air race to go halfway around the world.

I heard it all on Mrs Banks's wireless at 7 pm this evening, thanks to the superintendent of Fannie Bay Gaol, who allowed the broadcaster the use of his telephone line. When he talked about the bells in Adelaide, it gave me goosebumps.

The Smith brothers are the first pilots to fly 11,500 miles across the world. They did it in 135 flying hours and it took twenty-seven days and twenty hours, arriving four hours before the deadline. The wireless broadcaster said that their fuel tanks were so close to empty, their plane almost fell into Darwin.

Considering how big Australia is, George says it's a marvel they found Darwin at all. But I reckon the people cheering and waving their black umbrellas showed them the way.

The broadcaster, whose voice got higher and higher the more excited he became, described how there were so many women and children gathering in the Police Paddock that the police had to hold them back. They warned them that the Vickers Vimy bomber might skim along the ground at 100 miles per hour and that its propeller could cut a human in two without the aviator feeling the jolt.

Next we heard the sound of an aircraft engine and loud cheering, and we all cheered too, until Mrs Banks told us to hush so we could hear the broadcaster describe how the aircraft had done a circuit overhead before slowly dropping to the airstrip, coming to a stop at the far end.

The broadcaster told us the fuel truck was pulling out to service the aircraft. Then I thought he would have a fit as he described the four grinning men, dressed in their military uniforms, climbing out of the Vickers Vimy's cockpit and jumping to the ground.

This was followed by such loud cheering by us that Mrs Banks had to hush us again so she could hear as the broadcaster began describing how the Smith brothers were being greeted by the Acting Administrator of the Northern Territory, the

Honourable Staniforth Smith, the Mayor of Darwin, and the Defence Department's representative, Flight Lieutenant Hudson Fysh, who handed them over fifty congratulation-filled telegrams.

The Smith brothers shook hands with everyone, waved to the crowd, and then retired to the house of the superintendent of the Fannie Bay Gaol for refreshments.

'While the famous Vickers Vimy,' said the broadcaster in an awed voice, 'is covered with a tarpaulin and pegged to the ground to stop any wind damage.'

I can't wait for them to reach Longreach. George says it could take two weeks with all the celebrations they will be invited to attend.

11 December 1919—Darwin

The Argus newspaper says that Ross and Keith Smith are being wined and dined all over Darwin, and that the celebrations will go on for as long as it takes to overhaul their aircraft, which could be a week.

It also gave the mix of fuel used by the Vickers Vimy. I thought you might be interested. It is 400 gallons of aviation spirit, 40 gallons of Wakefield castrol and 2 gallons of kerosene.

George said if he put that into Lizzie, he guarantees she would fly too.

Love, Jack.

14 December 1919—On their way

Dear Matt,

Everything is so exciting. The Smith brothers are on their way after only two days. *The Bulletin* says that two long lengths of telephone line had to be temporarily removed and two trees chopped down before the Smith brothers could take off from Darwin. I bet they were Winston Chong the market gardener's trees. I bet he is as mad about it as a cat with a tin tied to its tail. I will write and ask Sing Lu.

The Smith brothers are going to fly the Barkly Tablelands route to Longreach (our return route), not the Gulf route, which Mr Fysh and Mr McGinness so carefully mapped but which both thought was inappropriate.

There is a third route to Melbourne. It was flown by Captain Wrigley and Sergeant Murphy in a BE2E biplane. The flight took forty-six hours, they covered 2,500 miles, and they are the first pilots to cross the centre of Australia.

Back to the Smith brothers. They are going to

fly into Sydney. They said if they could fly over the Himalayas, they could easily fly over the Blue Mountains twice. Did you hear that Matt? So you will see them after all. Please remember every second and write to me about it.

Love, Jack.

15 December 1919—Duckfluff

Dear Matt,

I collected your and Mama's letters this afternoon and was pleased to read that you have started an aviation scrapbook as well. Did you see the story in the newspaper about Lieutenants Parer and McIntosh who have just taken off from London? They won't be in the race as it has already been won. But they are still brave.

I am sorry Mrs Wentworth is moving to Melbourne. Mama said she gave you a glowing reference, even though you broke so many ornaments.

But why did she have to mention your hair in her reference? No one mentions mine except Avery, who calls me carrot top. I get him back. He is growing hair on his top lip so I call him duckfluff.

16 December 1919—Christmas concert

Another letter from you. I am glad your Christmas concert was a success and that the church raised so much money.

I'm sorry to hear that Margo Tanner said that there were no such things as red-haired angels. You should have told her there were no such things as snobby, buck-toothed angels either, but I suppose tipping a cup of fruit punch over her halo and head was just as good. And I'll be interested to hear how long you keep your New Year's resolution of not losing your temper.

The newspapers say that after leaving Katherine, the Smith brothers had to land somewhere short of Newcastle Waters, and that a search party was about to go out and look for them when a message was received from Mr and Mrs Lewis, of the Newcastle Waters Cattle Station, saying that the aircraft and crew were fine.

Waiting for the winners to reach Longreach is so nerve-racking that Avery and I can't sit still, so we rode out to Lord Billy's again, this time to invite him to come with us to see the winners arrive.

Lord Billy said he wouldn't miss it for quids, especially as some of his mob have been cutting the grass to keep the airstrip smooth. Then he invited us to go on a *minyari* (named after the little bush mouse guardian of children).

A *minyari* is when the Elders take the children for a walkabout in the bush so that the children can learn the language of the night creatures. Lord Billy says that birds and animals have a night language that is different to the language they speak during the day, and a wise hunter must know both.

Avery and I learnt the sounds of the night birds, saw the red eyes of possums gleaming in the moonlight, and heard the musical croaks of the tree frogs, but we didn't hear any dingoes.

Lord Billy says dingoes are too crafty to howl during a *minyari* because they don't want anyone to learn their night language. He says dingoes are smarter than dogs, who long ago gave up their night language to live with men beside their fires.

On the way home the most amazing and scary thing happened. Avery, Billy and I saw a min min light. I write this quite calmly, Matt, but to tell the truth, Avery and I were scared stiff, and Billy's neck fur stood up like anteater's needles.

There we were pretending our bikes were Vickers Vimy bombers shooting down German Fokkers, with Billy howling, when suddenly a ball of shimmering light, glowing as brightly as a star, appeared ahead of us. We almost fell off our bikes with shock and Billy almost tumbled out of the bag I carry him in. Of course we stopped immediately, but then so did the light. Then, when we pedalled cautiously towards it, it moved off in front of us. It stayed there, floating along effortlessly, until we reached the first lighted lamppost, when it disappeared. Not fading or moving away. It simply turned itself off. Billy went crazy, barking at where it had been.

We have decided not to tell anyone except you and Lord Billy.

17 December 1919—New job

It looks like Avery and I won't be riding out to shantytown after work any more, because Avery has discovered a marvellous way to earn extra money to buy a motorbike.

This is Avery's money-making idea. In Longreach, it is considered unseemly for a woman to enter a hotel because of the rough speech of the men. So when the cattlemen bring their wives and daughters to town to do their Christmas shopping (or, in this case, to see the winners of the air race), the wives sit outside the pubs and swelter in their cars, while the men are inside under the fans, drinking and talking business.

If the women wish to have a cool lemon squash or a cup of tea they have to wait for their men to bring one out, or they must squeeze their car horns to remind the men that they are thirsty. A couple of the pubs have a roped-off area on their verandas, but when the men get yabbering, the women are forgotten.

So Avery goes to the cars, or verandas, and asks the women if they would like a drink. Then he goes into the bar and tells the husband that his missus or daughter requests a cup of tea or a lemon squash. The husband pays for the tea or lemon squash and gives Avery sixpence to take it out to his wife.

Avery has only been cuffed around the ears once since he started his new business. He has been rushed off his feet, racing from car and veranda to the bar, and from hotel to hotel, so he has asked me to become his partner.

Of course I said yes.

Love, Jack.

18 December 1919—Christmas presents

Dear Matt,

I've received your letter asking what I have bought everyone for Christmas and I am answering it before I go to work.

Your present is a secret, but I have bought Pa a

hand-carved boomerang, and Mama a pure wool scarf from the Methodist Mission ladies' stall. I also bought Billy a sheepskin rug for his kennel. Mrs Banks said the sheepskin will be a waste, as Billy will eat it, which will be a change, as he usually likes socks and under-drawers from the washing line.

Later

You will never believe it, Matt! I earned so many sixpences this afternoon that I shall be sending some money to Mama to help pay Mama's and Pa's back rent. Thank you for telling me how much it was. Mama didn't mention one word about being in debt. I am also saving up for a leather flying cap, one lined with rabbit fur, and a pair of flying goggles, just in case I ever get the chance to go up in an aircraft.

Oh, I almost forgot. Some good news and some sad news in the newspaper. The Smith brothers were missing for some time, but a telegram arrived from Camoweal saying that they had safely landed at a bore 20 miles west of Anthony's Lagoon. The aviators are hoping to reach Brunette Downs where there is a good engineering shop.

Now for the sad news, the last official contestant in the race has crashed. Captain Howell's and Lieutenant Fraser's aircraft was wrecked off Corfu, Greece, on 10 December. There were no survivors.

19 December 1919—They are coming

Everyone in Longreach is on tenterhooks awaiting the arrival of the Smith brothers.

The Longreach hotels are doing a roaring trade, as are Avery and myself, and the Women's Auxiliary is busy preparing a celebratory dinner for the pilots and all the top nobs of the town.

Later

Billy and I are in trouble. I don't know how, but Billy has learnt to sing. Avery suggested I take him to our lemon squash and tea job, as he would make us a fortune in tips. So I did. But the pub owners told me that if I didn't take the 'howling little mongrel' home, they'd shoot him. Now Billy spends each afternoon tied up in the washhouse to stop him from following me.

The first time Billy sang, all the schoolgirls who make up the church choir and who are practising to sing *God Save The King* and *Walzing Matilda* for the Smith brothers' arrival, came rushing out of the church to see if a dog had been run over. The choirmaster was livid.

I have been forbidden to take Billy anywhere near the Methodist Church ever again.

Now Billy has taken to singing along with the Salvation Army band which stands on the street corner near the hostel. As soon as the bass drum begins, his tail starts to wag, his ears perk up, and his throat throbs with lusty howls.

Mrs Banks says it has to stop. She is threatening to give him to a passing drover.

George says I'm not to worry; no self-respecting drover would take him.

20 December 1919—Ross and Keith Smith

I have been reading about the Smith brothers in *The Bulletin*. It's amazing how ordinary people can become famous.

For instance, Ross and Keith Smith were salesmen when the Great War started. Ross Smith immediately enlisted in the Third Light Horse Brigade and sailed off to Gallipoli and Egypt, where in 1916 he joined the Australian Flying Corps. Meanwhile, Keith Smith, after being rejected by the Australian Infantry Force for health reasons, sailed off to England where he was commissioned in the Royal Flying Corps.

Both men were exceptional horsemen. Which enforces what Mr McGinness said: 'All Defence Departments believe that if a chap can ride a horse then he can fly an aircraft.'

21 December 1919—Anthony's Lagoon

The Bulletin says that the Smith brothers have had to stop at Anthony's Lagoon to mend their propeller with fencing wire. There was a cartoon in the newspaper. It showed two bushies examining the Vickers Vimy and saying ''Ere, Bill, his engine's gone bung. Go and get that fencin' wire off the plough, and I'll fix it for him.'

I told Avery all about the death adders at Anthony's Lagoon. He shivered all over. He hates snakes.

Mrs Banks says I will have to gag Billy during the Christmas festivities. I told her that Billy was one of God's creatures. She said it made no difference and that if Billy went, she wouldn't, and then there would be hell to pay.

22 December 1919—Bullroarers

Avery and I have made bullroarers for when the Smith brothers arrive.

A bullroarer is a piece of wood with a hole in it (that's the hardest part). The wood is attached to a string. Blacks use their hair to make the string (we tried that but it didn't work because our hair is too short and too straight). The string goes through the wood and the bullroarer is swung round and round to produce a roaring sound.

Mrs Banks forbade us to swing our bullroarers near the hostel, so after our lemon squash and tea job, Avery and I went to the cemetery to try them out. We didn't mean to scare anyone. We were just pretending to be pilots during the Great War.

We were swinging our bullroarers and shouting, 'Shot you, you Hun,' when an old man talking to his wife's grave heard us. He got such a fright he ran all the way back to town to tell everyone that he'd heard and seen the ghosts of two dead soldiers. We have not told anyone it was us.

Posting this tomorrow.

Love, Jack.

23 December 1919—George's news

Dear Matt,

George has had wonderful news. It came in a letter from Mr McGinness which, unfortunately, was written before the Smith brothers flew in to Cloncurry, so there is no first-hand news about their landing there. But *The Bulletin* says that like everywhere else, Cloncurry's residents opened their doors and their hearts to the pilots.

Back to Mr McGinness's letter.

It seems that after we left him at the Post Office Hotel in Cloncurry, Mr McGinness got to know a Mr Fergus McMaster, a wealthy grazier and the chairman of the Anti-Cattleduffing Organisation of West Queensland. Mr McMaster was fording the Cloncurry River on his way to Devoncourt Cattle Station when the front axle of his automobile snapped.

Mr McGinness gave Mr McMaster a lift into Cloncurry in his automobile. Then, on finding all the garages shut because it was Sunday, Mr McGinness removed the tin wall of one of the garages, found an axle, drove Mr McMaster back to his automobile and helped fix it.

On the way, he told Mr McMaster about his aerial service idea, and how an air service would make the lives of the cattle station owners and the cattle buyers easier.

As soon as Mr McMaster's automobile was fixed, Mr McMaster (with Mr McGinness following) drove to see a friend of his, Mr Alexander Kennedy, to tell him about the proposed aerial service.

Mr Kennedy, who is eighty-three years old, said he would join Mr McMaster in putting money into the venture if he could be the first paying passenger. Mr McGinness said it was a deal.

With two shareholders on board, Mr McGinness wrote to ask George if he would be interested in becoming the company's first mechanic, working with their engineer, Flight Sergeant Arthur Baird.

He wrote that Arthur Baird was a self-made man, much like George, who had graduated as a chemical engineer with the highest marks ever recorded from a workingman's college. Not only was he a pilot, he could listen to an aircraft engine and know exactly what was wrong with it.

George got on his high horse after reading this and said perhaps Mr Baird wouldn't be interested in working with an ex-shearer, self-taught mechanic who'd left school at nine years of age.

I wish Mr McGinness had asked me. I would have jumped at the chance of working with Mr Baird. I would work for nothing.

George said he'd wait and see what the Smiths'

aircraft looked like before replying and that Winton wasn't a town he fancied moving to. But I think he is just pretending not to be interested. I think he is tickled pink to have been asked.

24 December 1919—Christmas Eve

This evening, after delivering tea and lemon squash, Avery, two other boys who have not gone back home for Christmas and myself, began decorating the hostel's Christmas tree.

It is a branch from the eucalyptus that grows outside our bedroom window. It's now covered in chains made from newspaper, and paper lanterns cut out from the coloured pages of magazines.

Your parcel and Mama and Pa's parcel are underneath, as is George's and Avery's. George is coming to Christmas dinner. I hope he likes the tartan cap I bought him, and that Avery likes the Brylcreem I got him to slick down his hair.

Avery is in love with Nancy McFarlane, one of the Methodist choir girls. He says that she says that slicked down hair shows he is a gentleman. I don't see why. Anyway, no amount of Brylcreem slicks my hair down.

25 December 1919—Two Christmas dinners

Thank you for the socks and thank Mama and Pa for the book on Rolls Royce aircraft engines. I hope you liked the Eau de Cologne 777 and that Mama liked her scarf and Pa his boomerang.

Mr Fysh posted me a leather-bound note book, which I intend to use to write down everything about aircraft engines and the aerial service, and Mr McGinness posted me a pair of airman's leather gloves. They're too big, but I will keep them forever.

Now to tell you about our Christmas dinners. Both of them.

Even though the temperature was almost at boiling point, Mrs Banks and the ladies of the Methodist Mission cooked the most delicious Christmas roast with potatoes, pumpkin and parsnip, and plum pudding and brandy custard. The plum puddings had thruppences and sixpences inside. Billy ate all the leftovers.

With our stomachs so full that Billy and I were waddling, George took us out to see Lord Billy. Then, although there was not one part of us that wasn't bulging with food, we sat down to a second Christmas dinner.

First came grilled white grubs (the size of George's index finger) called *parootra boobti*. Lord

Billy said he liked his grubs raw but that George and I could have them 'whitefella cooked' if we liked. Which we did. They tasted like nuts.

Next came baked-in-the-earth wallaby and some sliced-up corned beef from a tin, all eaten without cutlery or plates. Lord Billy said he had an enamel plate somewhere if I was fussed. I said I wasn't. I never thought I would eat wallaby again, but the blacks stuffed it with wild onion and it tasted much better than George's cooking.

Next came some hard biscuits made by the women from ground grass seeds found in ants' nests. The biscuits were soaked in bush honey, discovered that morning in a turkey-wash wattle. George said we were fortunate to eat traditional food, as the blacks often prefer to go to the shops and buy tinned food instead of hunting. After the biscuits, the children got to chew the waxy honeycomb. I got some too.

What a sticky, greasy mess we ended up. So we all stripped off our trousers—do not gasp, Matt, blacks do not care about clothing the way we do—and we all jumped into the irrigation ditch of a nearby market garden and had a water fight.

Now I am back at the hostel. Avery and I are lying in hammocks on the veranda, both full as googs.

I hope you, Mama and Pa have had as

wonderful a Christmas as I had. I missed you all, and I would have given up this wonderful Christmas to be with you if I could have.

Love, Jack.

26 December 1919—Boxing Day

Dear Matt,

The Smith brothers will be arriving tomorrow morning. The town is chock-a-block with people and automobiles driven to town by farmers who normally only come in every three months. The hotels are full and people are sleeping in the passageways, and many more are camped around the racecourse.

The feeling of excitement in Longreach is so intense that Mrs Banks said you could cut it with a knife.

Avery and I have decided to take our blankets and bullroarers to the racecourse tonight. We are going to sleep there so we will be the first to see the Vickers Vimy G-EAOU arrive tomorrow morning. Lord Billy is going to join us in the morning.

27 December 1919—The celebrations

I am writing this after the most exciting day of my life.

Avery and I were huddled in our blankets, having slept very little because of our excitement, when someone spotted a speck on the horizon. Up we jumped and began swinging our bullroarers while everyone cheered and cheered.

The speck grew larger, then, before our amazed eyes, there was the Vickers Vimy flying towards the bedsheet spread out on the airstrip. It circled around, did a wing-jiggle as a greeting, then came down 'as smooth as cream!' as the man next to us kept shouting, over and over.

We surged forward, although the police officer kept shouting, 'Watch the propeller! Watch the propeller!', which we did, as no-one wanted to lose their head.

Captain Smith got out first, then Lieutenant Smith, then Sergeants Bennett and Shiers. All four wore their military uniforms.

The four men received a rousing welcome. Especially from the ladies, who leapt out of their sulkies and motor cars, hitched up their long skirts and, hanging onto their straw hats, raced across the racecourse as fast as any man.

Everyone was so excited to see the aviators that they had a party right there on the airstrip. But

Avery and I had only been given half a day off, so we had to leg it back to town as fast as we could, or we would have been in strife.

We were jogging away from the airfield when I saw Lord Billy and his mob. They had stayed at what they thought was a safe distance from the roaring aircraft. I waved and Lord Billy waved back, then he pointed to the sky. High above the racecourse were two brown hawks circling in exactly the same manner as the Vickers Vimy.

Now I'm tired, but it was worth sleeping out for. I am sure I shall dream of Vickers Vimys tonight.

28 December 1919—Meeting the winners

I am so excited that I can hardly write. Today the owner of the Longreach Motor Company gave all the mechanics and apprentices a half day off, so George, Billy and I went to the airstrip on George's motorbike. Avery followed on his bicycle.

Everyone was crowding around the Vickers Vimy, but Mr Fysh had asked the Smith brothers to look out for George and me, so when we arrived, the crowd pushed us forward.

That's how I got to shake hands with the Smith brothers and Sergeants Bennett and Shiers. I even got to sit in the cockpit of their Vickers Vimy. It was only for a minute because so many other people wanted to sit in it, important people like the mayor. But it was the most wonderful, exciting feeling. I couldn't stop grinning at George who was holding a wriggling Billy.

George was very impressed with the aircraft, although he was a bit embarrassed with all the hand shaking. I just wanted to touch the aircraft all over.

The propeller is amazing! Its blades are made of polished wood and Mr McGinness is right, if you walked into them while they were turning, they would cut off your head.

Captain Smith said if we wanted to come back tomorrow, when there were fewer people about, he would show Avery, George and me the Vickers Vimy's engine and where they kept the bombs during wartime.

29 December 1919—My big decision

I'm writing this in bed by the light of a torch. Avery is asleep.

All day long, the Longreach Motor Company's workshop was abuzz with talk about aircraft, airstrips, propellers, wheels, aircraft tyres, and having to wear so much leather to keep warm when up in the air. By the time the afternoon's work was over, my head was spinning. But not spinning enough to stop me jumping on my bike and riding out to the racecourse with Avery to have a look at the Vickers Vimy's engine. George went by motorbike.

Captain Smith recognised me and immediately helped me up on to the aircraft's wing so that I could look inside the engine. I tell you, Matt, it is nothing at all like a Model T Ford's engine.

It was while I was staring into the Vickers Vimy engine, with Captain Smith pointing at this and that, that I made a momentous decision. The day my apprenticeship with the Longreach Motor Company is finished, I am going to apply to Mr Fysh and Mr McGinness to become an aircraft mechanic apprentice. I want to learn first-hand about aircraft engines.

When I told Avery of my decision he was gobstruck. Then he said he was going to do the same thing.

I didn't tell Avery the real reason for my wanting to become an aircraft mechanic, but I will tell you. I want to be a pilot like the Smith brothers, like Mr Fysh and Mr McGinness. I want to learn to fly, and if I become an aircraft mechanic then I will have to learn so I can hear what is wrong with the engine, like Mr Baird can.

When I told George my plan of becoming an aircraft mechanic, he said he thought it might be quite some time before Mr Fysh's and Mr McGinness's aerial service got off the ground. He laughed at his 'off the ground' joke.

Then he said, 'So we both might be waiting some time before we go to work for Mr Fysh and Mr McGinness again.'

That's the first inkling he has given that he will work for them. I knew he would. George loves a challenge.

30 December 1919—They have gone

The Smith brothers took off in the middle of the morning so I was not at the racecourse to see them off. But I saw them fly over the town.

I stood to attention in the street, along with all the mechanics and twelve lined-up Model T Fords. The mechanics waved their hats and pressed the Model T Fords' horns, and the owner of the Longreach Motor Company raised the Union Jack and the Australian flag on the company's flagpole.

It's a bigger let-down now they are gone than it was when George and I returned to Longreach. It's as if everything I have been waiting for, for so long, is over and done with.

Even teaching Avery to dance, so that he can dance with Nancy McFarlane tomorrow night at the New Year's Ball, hasn't brightened me up. Mrs Banks says you can't have the highs without the lows. I suppose she's right.

But I wish I'd asked Captain Smith more questions. Such as what was it like when he flew Lawrence of Arabia to Damascus? What was the scariest part of the air race, the stretch over the Himalayan Mountains or the stretch over the Burma jungles? And what was he going to do now, especially with the 10,000 pounds? Was he going to start his own aerial service like Mr Fysh and Mr McGinness were trying to do?

31 December 1919—New Year's Ball

I am writing this before Avery and I set off for the New Year's Eve Bachelors' and Spinsters' Ball.

Lord Billy is in the blacks' section of the hospital. I visited him this morning. George says Lord Billy is sick because he eats too much white flour and sugar. He certainly looked sick.

I told him that Mr Fysh said he'd take him up in their new Avro 504K when they get it. He'd be the first black man in Australia to fly.

Lord Billy didn't like the idea. He said, 'Each

tribe has him place. The birds have the air and we fellas have the earth. We fellas lend the birds the earth to land on but them bird fellas, him not lent us the air to fly in.'

Later—After the ball

Before we left for the dance, Mrs Banks got us all in the mood by playing the portable gramophone her family gave her for Christmas.

It is a fine piece of machinery, set inside a polished wooden box, with an amplifier in the front, a wind-up spindle on the side, and a turntable on top. Mrs Banks put a record on the turntable, wound up the spindle, then, as the record revolved she placed the needle into an outer groove, and hey presto! Music!

The ball was held at the Shire Hall. The ladies wore dresses bought from Buckley and Nunn's Country Catalogue and delivered through the mail, dark silk stockings, and beaded cloche hats over short wavy hairstyles. George says the hats look like pilots' helmets. He's right.

The men wore three-button suits, waistcoats, striped shirts, buttoned boots, and fancy silk ties, all bought from Cosimos.

On arriving at the hall, Mrs Banks danced with each of us. Then the Mission ladies danced with us, followed by the girls from the Methodist choir. Avery danced with Nancy McFarlane. He said he'd been waiting to dance with her for weeks. She is quite pretty, but not as pretty as Una Bloom of Burketown.

The music was played by The Jimmy Ah Foo Family Band. Jimmy Ah Foo played the saxophone, his wife played the piano, one son played the drums, the other son played the piano accordion, and his daughter played the tambourine. And yes, I did tie Billy up so he couldn't follow me and sing with the band. But I swear I could hear him howling, probably in protest.

At 10 o'clock we queued to fill our plates with freshly baked bread, salad, ham, turkey and oysters (brought in from Rockhampton in bags of ice). Outside, there were gallons of sugary tea and sugary milk coffee boiling in kerosene tins, and a dessert table covered in butterfly cream cakes, pink and chocolate lamingtons, coconut banana custard, cream sponge, plum pudding and bowls of freshly whipped cream.

I had a good time. I danced with Nancy McFarlane and afterwards she told Avery she liked me best. So I am not popular at the moment even though I told him I already had a girlfriend. Yes I am still writing to Una Bloom.

I have made three New Year's resolutions: to be

an aircraft mechanic; to fly in an aircraft; and to keep a record of Mr Fysh's and Mr McGinness's aerial service in the leather-bound notebook Mr Fysh gave me for Christmas, starting tomorrow.

Mr McGinness has gone to Sydney to try to find some shareholders. George thinks this will be difficult, especially after a minister stood up in Federal Parliament and said flying was sinful.

I asked George if he thought flying was sinful. He said it didn't matter what he thought. If the public regarded aeroplanes as suicide machines and freak shows, Mr McGinness would have an uphill battle.

Wish Mama and Pa a Happy New Year for me.

Love, Jack.

This notebook is for writing down information about Mr Fysh's and Mr McGinness's aerial service, and anything else to do with aircraft.

1 January 1920

Here is a list of regulations Mr Fysh has written out for the pilots who will work for the aerial service. Some are funny, especially the one about spurs.

1. Don't take an aircraft into the air unless you are satisfied it can fly.
2. Never leave the ground with the motor leaking.
3. Don't turn sharply when taxiing. Have someone lift the tail around for you, or you may flip over and land on your head.
4. When taking off, look at the ground for stray automobiles and up in the air for stray aircraft. You don't want to smash into one.
5. Carry handkerchiefs to wipe your goggles. Sleeves will not do.
6. No aircraft must taxi to land faster than a man can walk.
7. Do not trust altitude instruments. Learn to gauge altitude yourself.
8. Before landing, check there are no aircraft below you. You don't want to land on one.

9. Hedge-hopping, or fence-hopping, will not be tolerated. It frightens farmers and animals.
10. If flying against the wind when you would prefer to be flying with it, do not make a sharp turn, you may crash. Turn gently.
11. Pilots must not wear spurs while flying. They catch on the interior equipment of the aircraft.
12. If an emergency occurs while flying, land on anything flat as soon as possible. A road will do.

14 January 1920

I have been reading about some of the aircraft used during the Great War. The deadliest British aircraft was the single seat Sopwith Camel.

10 February 1920

For my fifteenth birthday, Mama and Pa sent me a book about W E Hart, the first man to hold an Australian pilot's licence. I am collecting a large aviation library.

Mr Hart bought a Bristol biplane and taught

himself to fly in 1911. In 1912 he challenged an American flier called Wizard Stone to a race from Sydney to Parramatta for the prize of 250 pounds. Hart won. It was Australia's first air race.

16 February 1920

Captain Smith's and Lieutenant Smith's Vickers Vimy arrived in Sydney yesterday. They intend to do the Sydney to Melbourne flight nonstop.

25 February 1920

Yesterday the Smith brothers landed on Melbourne's Flemington Racecourse. They had to land three times during their flight from Sydney.

They were greeted by a crowd of people and congratulated by Prime Minister Billy Hughes and the Governor-General, who presented them with a cheque for 10,000 pounds sterling.

1 March 1920

It has just been announced in the newspapers that King George V of England will give Captain Smith and Lieutenant Smith a knighthood each. Which means they will be called Sir Ross Smith and Sir Keith Smith from now on.

9 March 1920

When we were driving back from Darwin, Mr McGinness talked about what could go wrong with an aircraft when flying. I have made a list of what he said.

1. If the undercarriage is weak, the aircraft may break up on landing.
2. Forced landings because of engine failure are dangerous. So is flying in darkness or bad weather, or when overflying the runway.
3. If you fly through a telephone line, rabbit-proof fence or strike a railway line, the aircraft may end up doing a nosedive.
4. Landing on the aircraft's nose can cause the aircraft to somersault and land on its back.
5. If a tyre bursts on landing, or a wheel-rim is bogged in dirt, the aircraft can swerve dangerously and flip over, causing it to break up.
6. If you take off in temperatures over 100

degrees Fahrenheit, there could be air turbulence and the aircraft can overturn.

7. If you are taking off from a too-short runway and you stall, you could hit the aerodrome's fence, a row of trees, or a telegraph wire.
8. If when taking off or landing the tail skid catches on a concealed rock, or the wheels run into a ditch, the aircraft can tilt onto its nose.
9. On the ground, heavy winds can blow an untethered aircraft onto its beam-end. The pilot must climb out of the cockpit onto the aircraft's nose to weigh it down.
10. Finally, the pilot's golden rule. If you have an accident, get back into the air as soon as possible.

Mr McGinness said none of the above would result in the pilot being badly hurt. He says flying is not dangerous. Crashing is the dangerous bit.

12 March 1920

While fetching tea for two ladies waiting in a car outside the Federal Hotel, I overheard one lady say that she'd heard from her cousin in Darwin that Mr Fysh would soon be returning to Longreach.

There are three ways of leaving Darwin: the monthly boat which sails around Cape York through the Great Barrier Reef to Rockhampton and Brisbane; overland to Adelaide by horse or camel; or the Barkly Tablelands route, which is the one I think Mr Fysh will take, even though it is the wrong time of year and it will be raining every day.

1 May 1920

Today, Avery and I marched in the May Day March. We marched behind the United Mechanics' banner. When the men went off to the hotel to celebrate a holiday, Avery and I went home to read and test each other on our knowledge of Australian aviators. One day we will march under an Aircraft Mechanics' banner. One day we will be aircraft mechanics.

24 May 1920

Important information about how aircraft fly from an aircraft mechanics' manual.

There are four main factors (lift, weight, thrust and drag) that help an aircraft stay up in the air.

1. Lift makes the aircraft go up.

2. Weight pulls the aircraft down.
3. Thrust makes the aircraft go forward.
4. Drag pulls the aircraft backwards.

Lift and weight must be equal to keep the aircraft in the air; thrust and drag must be equal before the engine can overcome the aircraft's weight and drag and allow it to fly forwards.

For example, if the lift and weight aren't equal, the aircraft will not get off the ground. If the thrust of the engine isn't more than the drag of an aircraft's weight through the air, then the aircraft will fall out of the sky.

George says, if it is the drag that holds the aircraft back, then why can't an aircraft's body be smoother and sleeker like a bird's body? And why can't its wheels be folded up inside its fuselage to diminish the drag they cause? He says that with less drag the aircraft could go faster, and that birds don't fly with their legs hanging down or their heads sticking up. He says it is the same with automobiles; they will have to become sleeker and lower to the ground if they are to go faster.

He's right. But the idea of an aircraft flying without its wheels in place, in case of a forced landing, is revolutionary. Also, if automobiles are going to be lower to the ground, how will the women, with their big automobile hats and scarves, fit into them?

3 June 1920

No-one knows when Mr Fysh will reach Longreach, as the Gulf Track is a mud pit, and there will be no horses to pull them out, as no self-respecting drover would take his horses across the Northern Territory or north Queensland at this time of year.

6 June 1920

On 31 May Captain Hubert Hinkler set off from England for Australia. He reached Turin, Italy, setting the record for the longest nonstop flight ever. The newspaper said he took off wearing a three-piece suit and a bowler hat, and that on landing in Italy the Italians gave him a hero's welcome.

9 June 1920

More hints for safety of aircraft, copied from another aircraft mechanics' manual.

In every 4-gallon can of petrol there is a small amount of water. This water makes the aircraft's engine cough and its propellers stall, or worse, spin backwards, causing the aircraft to fall into a spin and crash. This is why all petrol must be strained.

If a strainer, which is made of chamois leather, is not available, a felt hat will do. Water is lighter than oil, so it will soak into the material and the material can be wrung out as you are straining.

30 July 1920

Mr Fysh has finally returned to Longreach. He said he left Darwin for Cloncurry on 27 May, with a Mr Hogan, a Mr Ross, and Mr Lynott (the Borroloola hotel owner who gave me Billy). They had five punctures on the first day, forty-one during the entire trip, and they drove half the distance with the tyres stuffed with grass and sugar sacking.

About 70 miles outside of Borroloola they hit an ant hill and Mr Lynott and Mr Hogan had to walk back to the nearest lagoon with Mr Fysh's gun (the only one the party had brought with them), while Mr Fysh and Mr Ross trudged the 70 miles to Borroloola with only a billy of water between them.

It took them three days to reach Borroloola and three days for a team of horses to return to Mr Lynott and Mr Hogan, who'd existed for the week on roasted galahs.

The Model T Ford was towed to Borroloola and mended, but it only lasted 40 miles, conking out at McArthur River Station. Fortunately the station owner was driving to Cloncurry the next day.

On their way to Cloncurry they were drenched by the last summer rains and stranded on the wrong side of Wills Creek. This turned out to be the property of Mr Kennedy, the second shareholder of their proposed aerial service. Mr Fysh made Mr Kennedy's acquaintance, and once Wills Creek subsided, Mr Kennedy and Mr Fysh continued on to Cloncurry, where they met up with Mr McGinness and Mr McMaster and had their first shareholders' meeting. The main subject was how to get more paying shareholders.

Mr Fysh described Mr McMaster as a stubborn teetotaller Scotsman, and Mr Kennedy as one of the first pioneers to tackle the wilderness while the fierce Kalkadoons were still fighting settlers.

1 August 1920

Today I asked Mr Fysh if I could become an aircraft mechanic apprentice with his aerial service.

I held my breath after I had spoken for fear he would make fun of me. But he said that he knew I was keen. So as soon as I have finished my automobile apprenticeship, he would be very pleased, as one of the owners of the Queensland and Northern Territory Aerial Service Company (that's the name he and Mr McGinness have given their aerial service) to take me on as an apprentice.

He said it so casually that at first I didn't believe my ears. It had taken so long for me to get up the courage to ask, and there he was saying yes straight away.

3 August 1920

Mr Fysh and Mr McGinness are going to Sydney to buy two aircraft.

27 August 1920

Mr McGinness is back from Sydney. He came into the workshop to tell everyone that ten days ago, he and Mr Fysh bought two Avro 504K biplanes.

The aircraft cost 1,500 pounds each. Mr McMaster put up 1,000 pounds; Mr Templeton, Mr Thompson, Mr Campbell, and Mr O'Rouke put up another 1,000 pounds between them; Mr Fysh put up 500 pounds; and Mr McGinness put up 1,000 pounds. Mr McGinness asked George if he was interested in becoming a shareholder.

George wasn't too keen. He only earns 4 pounds a week and it all goes into his saving fund for his old age. Mr McGinness said that was the problem, people were afraid to invest for fear of losing all their savings, even though he assures them that it is as sound an investment as money in the bank.

28 August 1920

I looked up the Avro 504K biplane in Mr McGinness's aircraft book. It is 29 feet long with a 36 foot wingspan, an open cockpit, and passenger area that seats two. It is considered more efficient than the BE2E.

Mr McGinness said it could hardly be less efficient or it wouldn't get off the ground.

3 September 1920

Mr McGinness and Mr Fysh have shortened the name of their Queensland and Northern Territory Aerial Service to Q.A.N.T.A.S.

They are planning to make enough money from joy-riding to keep the aircraft in the air until they get the government mail contract. Mr Fysh says Captain Smith and Lieutenant Smith are doing joy-riding down in Adelaide, and that Kingsford Smith is doing the same thing in the United States.

George thinks joy-riding won't catch on because everyone is yabbering about an aircraft crash that happened down south; no-one is going to pay to be killed no matter how thrilling it sounds.

6 September 1920

A draft of a pamphlet Mr McGinness has prepared to advertise Q.A.N.T.A.S. says that the service will include: joy-riding; loop the looping; taxiing of bookies to race meetings; shotgun hunting of bush turkey from the air; and the dropping of *billet doux* (love letters) and chocolates from bachelors wishing to woo sweethearts living on distant stations.

It also advises prospective passengers that flying caps, dustcoats and goggles are not necessary; that movements in the passenger seat will not affect the aircraft's balance; and people with weak hearts, or mothers and babies need not fear.

12 September 1920

Mr Fysh has been appointing agents in all the towns they intend flying to.

Each agent must prepare an airstrip close to his town. It must be a rock-free level space of 1,200 yards long by 800 yards wide, and it must face into the prevailing winds, with the vicinity clear of telegraph wires, fences and ditches.

When an aircraft is due, the agent must place a white bedsheet in the middle of the airstrip and light a smoky fire to indicate wind direction. They must write out tickets, take money, offer a thermos of tea to the passengers while the aircraft is refuelling, and look after the wobbly-legged joy-riders when they alight. They do not get paid, but in return for their work they get free flights.

In Europe, wealthy people who own their own planes and employ their own pilots often take their dogs flying with them. Their dogs wear goggles and leather caps exactly like their owners. I wonder if Billy would like to fly?

4 October 1920

I have just read that the Avro 504K biplane's rotary engine is considered unreliable in hot weather. I immediately went in search of Mr McGinness to ask him about it. Mr McGinness told me they are having their two Avro 504Ks fitted with 100 horsepower, water-cooled vertical six-cylinder engines, which will not be affected by Queensland heat.

10 October 1920

Mr Fysh and Mr McGinness are very disappointed at receiving a telegram that says they can only get one Avro 504k. So they have ordered an Avro triplane instead. A triplane carries four passengers but costs twice as much as an Avro 504k.

This is a worry, as Mr McGinness and Mr Fysh are so broke they are living on Rex camp pie sandwiches and Bushells tea. They are still being invited to every cattle station for miles around, though. George says it's because the station owners are wanting to marry off their daughters.

1 November 1920

Frank L Roberts has piloted the first air flight to inspect a mob of sheep, out Darr River way. He had two buyers with him. Payment for the flight depended on the sale of the sheep. The sheep were sold and the full fee paid. Mr McGinness is adding 'inspection of sheep and cattle' to his publicity pamphlets.

20 November 1920

Mr McGinness and Mr Fysh are back from Brisbane where they went to register Q.A.N.T.A.S. They met up with a friend of Reverend Warren when they were there.

His name is Reverend John Flynn. He said that as there are only two doctors in the millions of square miles of the outback, their aerial service would be a godsend if it meant sick people could be flown to the nearest hospital.

Mr McGinness added 'taxiing the sick to and from hospital' to Q.A.N.T.A.S.'s publicity pamphlets.

29 December 1920

Mr Charles Knight, a stock and station agent, has bought a BE2E. He wants Mr Fysh to fly it from Sydney to Longreach for him and to teach him how to fly. Mr Fysh has agreed to do so if he can fly the BE2E up at the same time as Mr McGinness flies up their Avro 504K.

1 January 1921—Longreach

Dear Matt,

Yes, I had a wonderful Christmas. Yes, I received your presents. And yes I went to the Bachelors' and Spinsters' Ball again. But none of that is as exciting as the news I have to tell you.

I am to come to Sydney before the end of my apprenticeship. Mrs Banks is closing the hostel for two weeks so she can go to Brisbane to see her sick parents, so Mr Fysh and Mr McGinness asked the owner of the Longreach Motor Company if he would release me from training for two weeks.

I am to travel down by train with Mr Fysh and Mr McGinness. I shall stay a week with Mama, Pa and you. Then, and this is the breathtakingly exciting part (the part I can hardly write about for fear it won't come true), I am to fly almost all the way back with Mr McGinness in the Avro 504K. I am also to guard both aircraft at the different towns we will stop at on the way back.

I would have flown back with Mr Fysh, even though he has only ever landed an aircraft once, but Mr Fysh is to bring back Mr Baird, the engineer.

At Barcaldine, Mr Baird and I will catch the train to Longreach, and Mr McMaster and Mr Templeton, two important shareholders, will take my place in the Avro 504K to fly the last part into

Longreach and Winton. Mr Knight will fly in his own aircraft with Mr Fysh. They will be Q.A.N.T.A.S.'s first passengers, although it's not a proper scheduled flight.

Isn't it just the most amazing thing, Matt? I can't sleep for thinking about it. Avery says if I don't stop twisting about he'll throttle me. Avery is going to look after Billy. He is a good mate even though he says he is green all over with jealousy.

Love, Jack.

25 January 1921—Singleton

Dear Matt,

What a wonderful week it was seeing you all again. How healthy Pa looks; how happy Mama is that he has work at the tramyards; and how tall you have grown. When did you become taller than me?

Sydney and Leichhardt haven't changed a bit. But you have. You have become a genius. I can't believe you know so much about aircraft design, construction and maintenance. How did you learn the names of every aerodrome in the world? Not to mention knowing all the famous pilots, their aircraft and the distances they have flown.

Of course I agree with you wanting to become a pilot like me. Why shouldn't you? There are female pilots in Europe. We will be pilots together.

I'm so glad you came to the Mascot Aerodrome to see me off. Could you see that I was wearing Mr McGinness's air force flying jacket, rabbit-lined cap, goggles, gloves, and far-too-big leather overalls?

You have no idea how nervous I felt about leaving the ground. My hands were shaking so much that after I climbed into my seat I couldn't buckle myself in. Mr McGinness had to do it for me. He said that everyone was nervous on their first flight, and that everyone must be tightly buckled into their seat in case the aircraft goes into a spin, or a loop and they fall out. This bit of information did not make me feel any better.

After the chocks were removed from the front and back wheels, Mr McGinness started the engine with the inside crank handle, and we taxied to the far end of the airstrip. Here we turned slowly so as not to tip over. I think I could still see you waving.

With a shout of, 'Here goes mate', Mr McGinness opened up the throttle, pushed the joystick forward, and off we went, pelting down the runway.

The faster we went the more the Avro 504K shuddered and the louder the whirling propellers thrummed. The engine roared, the wing wires twanged and whistled from the wind, and my scarf flew out behind me. Then, as the Cooks River and the boundary fence rushed to meet us and my stomach hit my boots, Mr McGinness pulled back the joystick and, after an initial jolt, we were suddenly airborne.

Flying is a wonderful feeling. Being so high is the most exciting thing in the world.

The Parramatta River, Port Jackson and North and South Heads were spread out below like a huge map. I don't think anyone should arrive in Sydney any other way than by air. I could see the ferry boats on their way to Manly; the summer bushfires in the Blue Mountains; and far behind us, Mr Fysh and Mr Baird in Mr Knight's BE2E.

Within an hour, the storm that had been threatening to set in did so, and we were soon flying blind, buffeted by winds from all directions. That was when we lost contact with Mr Fysh and Mr Baird.

Later, when Mr Fysh and Mr Baird joined us at Singleton, we discovered what had happened to them.

Deep in the rain clouds and flying blind, all Mr Fysh had to guide him were a dodgy compass, that swung erratically with the motion of the BE2E; an inclinometer, that measured the inclination of the aircraft to the horizontal (if Mr Fysh had known where the horizon was); and a speed indicator, which he prayed would not drop below 25 miles per hour or the engine would stall and they would fall. How far down, they had no idea.

Within seconds of losing visibility, the BE2E stalled and entered a spin. It was at that moment that the clouds below them broke, and they saw a valley full of mining pitheads. Recovering from the spin, Mr Fysh landed on an uphill slope, coming to a halt outside a miner's cottage.

The miner's wife (who didn't seem at all surprised at seeing an aircraft and two men wearing goggles land in her front yard) invited them in for a cup of tea.

When the clouds lifted they turned the BE2E around, cleared some bushes away, and took off downhill, just missing an electric power line.

1 February 1921—Moree

We landed at the Moree airstrip like two eagles swooping on rabbits. The Mayor of Moree was waiting to shake our hands and hand over a telegram from Mr McMaster to Mr McGinness.

The telegram said there were 3½ tons of petrol and three cases of engine oil stored in Longreach awaiting our arrival.

Both the Singleton and the Moree councillors

welcomed us with open arms and a great many curious spectators came to see their first aircraft. We have been besieged by newspaper reporters wanting to interview the owners of Q.A.N.T.A.S. and wanting to know if this first flight means there will be a regular service.

It is very exciting being part of all of this, Matt. I wish you could be here too.

I am having a difficult job keeping all the curious hands off the aircraft.

Love, Jack.

3 February 1921—St George

Dear Matt,

After spending the night in Moree, we flew to St George, where we have been for a couple of days because Mr Baird insisted on attending to a fault that could cause problems.

Every day the airstrip is crowded with people. Mr McGinness is worried that on-the-spot-repairs will not instil confidence in prospective customers. But Mr Fysh says it shows how careful the staff of Q.A.N.T.A.S. are.

4 February 1921—Charleville

We left St George this morning. When we landed in Charleville (the first town to clear its own airstrip for our arrival) the town's ambulance was waiting. Mr McGinness thanked the driver, who offered to drive us into town, but the mayor was waiting to be photographed with the two pilots.

I was photographed spinning the propeller and standing beside the Avro's tail. I wonder if I will be in a Sydney newspaper?

I am getting used to landing and taking off and have not been airsick once.

5 February 1921—Blackall

We have reached Blackall, but not speedily enough for Mr McGinness. He believes that if an aircraft could fly at night, it would cut travelling time in half. He says night flying won't happen until more reliable compasses are invented, because at the moment a pilot must be able to look down to see where he is.

But I reckon if a pilot was taught to navigate by the stars, he could fly at night. Although then there would have to be two pilots per aircraft so one could sleep, which would mean bigger aircraft, and if they got too big, they might not be able to leave the ground.

6 February 1921—Barcaldine

On approaching Barcaldine, the air was so clear that from a great distance I could see a row of ant-sized people standing in front of automobiles, pony traps, buggies and wagons. It looked as if the whole of Barcaldine was there.

Mr McGinness landed the Avro 504K without a bump. Then he taxied to one side so that Mr Fysh could land the BE2E. They were two perfect landings. It isn't always that easy.

Mr McMaster, Mr Templeton and Mr Knight rushed over to shake hands and to be photographed, then they all piled into the waiting vehicles and drove straight to the bar of the Shakespeare Hotel to celebrate. I remained behind to watch the aircraft.

As I wrote before, Mr Baird and I are to take the train from now on. Mr McMaster and Mr Templeton will fly into Longreach and Winton with Mr McGinness, and Mr Knight will fly in his newly acquired BE2E with Mr Fysh.

Later

I am on the train travelling west from Barcaldine. I will arrive an hour or so after the aircraft land in Longreach.

I would have loved to have flown with them and to have seen Avery's face as I climbed out of the Avro's passenger seat.

Still, nothing can take away the excitement or the magic of having flown from Sydney to Barcaldine, though there were times that my heart almost stopped and my hands gripped the edge of the aircraft so tightly they ached. But even the fear is exciting. I can't wait to fly again.

Much later

The following is what Avery told me. When the Avro and BE2E landed on the Longreach racecourse, George, Mrs Banks, the boys from the hostel, the waitresses from Cosimos, all the townspeople, and many more from miles around were there to greet them.

Mr McGinness leant out of the Avro's cockpit and waved wildly to everyone as he landed perfectly on the soft slushy ground. Mr Fysh simply smiled as he swung the BE2E around and taxied back, his tyres already coated with mud. Mr

McGinness's passengers, Mr McMaster and Mr Templeton, were laughing as they climbed out of their seats but Mr Knight did not look well as he left the BE2E.

I arrived at Longreach not long after they landed, claimed my bicycle, which Avery had left at the station for me, and pedalled as fast as I could, which wasn't easy as the mud clung in lumps to my tyres and spokes.

I had no sooner arrived at the crowded airstrip, when a flash of lightning split the sky, and the wind and rain started.

Had it not been for so many willing hands, including mine, holding down the bucking aircraft, I am sure the wind, that had already thrown them on their beam ends once, would have done so again and again, and they would have been badly damaged.

7 February 1921—Last stretch

Today the Avro 504K, piloted by Mr McGinness, with Mr McMaster and Mr Templeton as passengers, took off for Winton. Behind them flew Mr Fysh in Mr Knight's BE2E, with a very white-faced Mr Knight sitting in the back seat.

Avery and I leant on our bike handles and

watched as the aircraft circled over the town, gaining height with each circle until they were two tiny dots in the sky. Then we pedalled back to town as we were late for work.

8 February 1921—Changes all round

I have five pieces of wonderful news.

The first is that the shareholders of Q.A.N.T.A.S. have decided to move their headquarters from Winton to Eagle Street in Longreach, because Longreach is more central and the railhead is here. So they will be just down the road.

The second is that on his return flight from Winton, Mr Fysh missed Longreach by 20 miles. On landing, Mr Knight vowed that he would never fly in an aircraft again. He has sold his BE2E to Q.A.N.T.A.S. for a very cheap price.

The third is that Q.A.N.T.A.S. has been awarded the contract for a mail and passenger service between Charleville and Cloncurry.

The fourth is that Avery's tea and lemon squash business has become so lucrative, we have both saved enough money to buy a second-hand Douglas motorbike each. Now I can get out to the airstrip without depending on George.

And the fifth is . . . the best bit of news. As I

only have a couple of months left of my apprenticeship, and as I have already passed the exams, the boss mechanic and owner of Longreach Motor Company have agreed to release me so I can start work at Q.A.N.T.A.S. immediately. Although both of them said it was a bit rich losing two good men in one month.

They mean George. He has given in his notice, and will begin working with Mr Baird from next week.

Love, Jack.

9 February 1921—My plan

Dear Matt,

Remember the plan I've been telling you about for almost two years? Well here it is.

Mr Baird said I have an aptitude for aircraft engines and he wished there were more apprentices like me. So I suggested that he apprentice my twin, who was a far smarter mechanic than me.

Mr Baird talked to Mr Fysh and Mr McGinness about it, and they have all agreed to give you a go.

So, dear Matt, please find enclosed sufficient money for a train ticket to Longreach. How you get Mama to let you go will be up to you, but I know you will, as there is a no more determined girl than you on this earth. Pa already knows my plan. I told him when I was in Sydney. He says it's worth the gamble and that he has faith in you. He thinks you are a genius too.

Once on the train you are to put on the clothes I left with you. Sorry if my trousers are a bit short, but you will insist on growing faster than me. Then you must cut off your hair so you'll look like a boy (it gets in the way when your head is in an engine anyway). When you've proven your worth, which you will within a couple of weeks, you can tell them that you are a girl.

The next move will be up to Mr McGinness, Mr Fysh and Mr Baird. But I am sure they will keep you, as Mr McGinness is always talking about European women pilots and engineers.

Mrs Banks has agreed to keep the fact that you are a girl a secret, as she cannot see why women can't get grease under their fingernails if they want to. She is a bit of a suffragette.

She is giving you the room at the back on one condition, that you share it with Billy. Billy has rejected his kennel so vocally that the neighbours are complaining. Mrs Banks says Mama is to write to her if she has any worries.

So please come. The worst thing that can happen is that you become a housemaid again. The best is that you become the first female aircraft mechanic and perhaps the first aviatrix in Australia.

Not only that, I am dying to introduce you to Avery, Lord Billy, Mrs Banks and Billy.

Your loving brother, Jack.

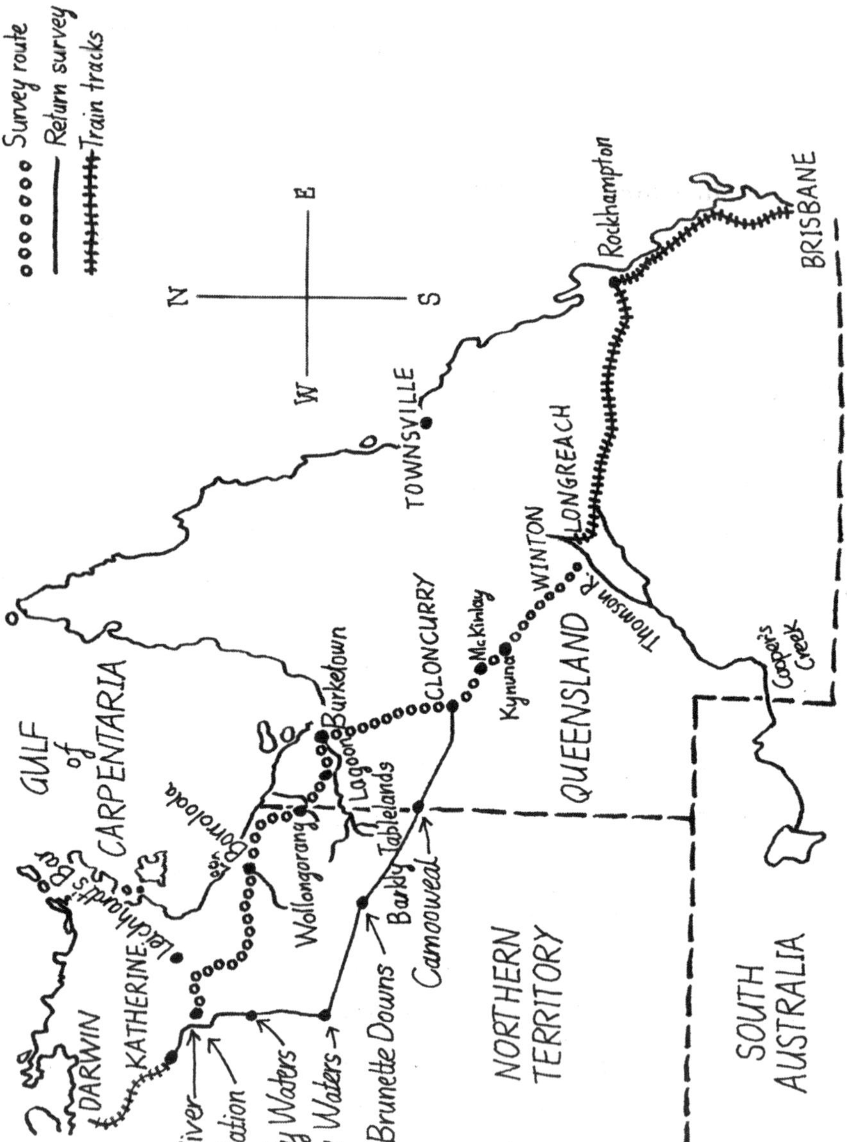

Survey route
Return survey
Train tracks
N
S
E
W
GULF of CARPENTARIA
DARWIN
KATHERINE
Leichhardt's
Doomadgee
Wollongorang
Lagoon
Burketown
CLONCURRY
McKinlay
Kynuna
WINTON
LONGREACH
Thomson R.
TOWNSVILLE
Rockhampton
BRISBANE
Cooper's Creek
Roper River
Elsey Station
Daly Waters
Newcastle Waters
Brunette Downs
Barkly Tablelands
Camooweal
NORTHERN TERRITORY
QUEENSLAND
SOUTH AUSTRALIA

HISTORICAL NOTE

In March 1919, Billy Hughes, Prime Minister of Australia, offered a 10,000 pound prize for the first Australians to fly from England to Australia. The flight was to take no more than twenty-eight days.

Flight Lieutenants W Hudson Fysh and Paul 'Ginty' McGinness immediately contacted Sir Samuel McCaughey, a millionaire industrialist, to ask for financial assistance. During the war, Sir Samuel McCaughey had presented No. 1 Squadron of the Australian Flying Corps with a Bristol fighter which both men had flown in, so they were sure he would support their endeavour.

Sir Samuel McCaughey agreed to finance them, so they contacted their old Flight Sergeant, Arthur Baird, and the three prepared to sail to London. Unfortunately Sir Samuel McCaughey died before they left Australia, forcing them to pull out of the race.

Lieutenants Fysh and McGinness then accepted an offer from the Defence Department to survey the northern Australian race route for the successful competitors, while Flight Sergeant Baird returned to his Melbourne garage business.

Fysh's and McGinness's fifty-one day journey

from Longreach, Queensland, to Katherine, Northern Territory, began on 18 August 1919. During this time the idea of an air service, linking all the western Queensland railheads with Katherine and Darwin, was born.

The England–Australia air race was won by Captain Ross Smith and Lieutenant Keith Smith, from South Australia, on 10 December 1919. At the time, Captain Smith was the most decorated aviator in Australian history.

On landing in Darwin, the Smith brothers were greeted by Lieutenant Fysh. Captain Smith had been Lieutenant Fysh's Commanding Officer in Egypt.

Meanwhile Paul McGinness had secured the backing needed for their aerial service from a grazier called Fergus McMaster, the then chairman of the new Anti-Cattleduffing Association of Queensland.

With the help of Mr McMaster and his friends, Mr Templeton, Mr Thompson, Mr Campbell, and Mr O'Rourke, the Queensland and Northern Territory Aerial Service (Q.A.N.T.A.S.) was registered in Brisbane on 16 November 1920.

Qantas is the second oldest airline in existence. KLM Royal Dutch Airlines, which was registered a mere thirteen months earlier, is the oldest.

Thanks to:

Mrs Carmen Brook, Head librarian, Longreach Library.

Ms Kathy MacDonald, Longreach Motors, Longreach.

Elaine Britton, Acacia Downs, Longreach.

Mitchell Library, Research Department.

Sciences Library, University of New South Wales.

Powerhouse Museum, Sydney, Research Department.

Dorothy Basili, University of New South Wales.

Mr Adrian Ryan, Ford Discovery Centre, Geelong.

Mr George Roberts, Qantas Museum, Mascot.

Mr Ron Yeates, Veteran Car Club of Australia (NSW) and Model T Ford Club of Australia.

Qantas Museum, Longreach.

Mr Ken Williams, Australian Rail Resource Centre.

Mr Stuart Zlotkowski, Wollogorang Cattle Station.

Kim and Tim Trad, owners of the Burketown Hotel, Burketown.

Norma Kinitavaki, Davis Morris, Jayne McKenzie, John D'Riago, Chris Targett.

Aviation Heritage Centre, Winnellie, Darwin.

Darwin Public Library, Government House, Darwin.

Northern Territory Archives.

Leanne Thorpe, Northern Territory Library Services.

Bob Alford, Heritage Consultant, Darwin.

PATRICIA BERNARD

Patricia Bernard left Australia when she was nineteen. During the next twenty years she sailed up the Nile, worked in Berlin during the closing of the Berlin wall, met Mohammed the Fifth of Morocco in the Sahara Desert, travelled through Alaska in winter in a sports car, fell in love with a Spanish matador, married in Jamaica, hitch-hiked with her one-year-old daughter around Japan and Korea just after the Korean War, became stranded on the Niagara Falls Bridge without a passport, visited Lhasa in Tibet, was among the first Australians to visit China in the seventies, and was the first NSW resident given a visa for Cuba.

She has worked and travelled in many places: the USA, Scandinavia, Thailand, Belgium, Mexico, Guatemala, France, Zimbabwe, Botswana, Germany, Czech Republic, Easter Island, Vietnam and Laos, Cambodia, Reunion, Mauritius and Madagascar. She intends seeing all the other countries she hasn't yet seen before she falls off the planet.

Patricia lives in Sydney in a convict-built house. She has three daughters, one son, and two fluffy silky terrier watchdogs. She loves travel, science fiction, children and cinema.